"I leave the opposite sex of the married kind alone!"

Cheyne paused, then finished, "Unlike you."

What made her do it Jolene wasn't sure, but the slap which had been on its way to him all day suddenly got delivered.

She felt his iron grip on her arms. "No," she cried, then suddenly Cheyne's warm and attractive mouth was over hers, effectively shutting her up.

As she pushed herself furiously away, Cheyne ground out, "That is not the way to get a promotion."

"Well, I sure as Henry am not going to go to bed with you to get it!" she shot back.

"You should get the chance!" he told her arrogantly, stalking away. Had she really hit the chairman of Templeton's? Had the chairman really kissed her?

Jessica Steele first tried her hand at writing romance novels at her husband's encouragement two years after they were married. She fondly remembers the day her first novel was accepted for publication. "Peter mopped me up, and neither of us cooked that night," she recalls. "We went out to dinner." She and her husband live in a hundred-year-old cottage in Worcestershire, and they've traveled to many fascinating places—such as China, Japan, Mexico and Denmark—that make wonderful settings for her books.

Books by Jessica Steele

HARLEQUIN ROMANCE
2850—BEYOND HER CONTROL
2861—RELATIVE STRANGERS
2916—UNFRIENDLY ALLIANCE
2928—FORTUNES OF LOVE
2964—WITHOUT LOVE
2982—WHEN THE LOVING STOPPED
3011—TO STAY FOREVER
3041—FAREWELL TO LOVE

HARLEQUIN PRESENTS
717—RUTHLESS IN ALL
725—GALLANT ANTAGONIST
749—BOND OF VENGEANCE
766—NO HOLDS BARRED
767—FACADE
836—A PROMISE TO DISHONOUR

Don't miss any of our special offers. Write to us at the following address for information on our newest releases.

Harlequin Reader Service
901 Fuhrmann Blvd., P.O. Box 1397, Buffalo, NY 14240
Canadian address: P.O. Box 603,
Fort Erie, Ont. L2A 5X3

FROZEN ENCHANTMENT

Jessica Steele

Harlequin Books

TORONTO • NEW YORK • LONDON
AMSTERDAM • PARIS • SYDNEY • HAMBURG
STOCKHOLM • ATHENS • TOKYO • MILAN

Original hardcover edition published in 1989
by Mills & Boon Limited

ISBN 0-373-03065-7

Harlequin Romance first edition July 1990

CHAPTER ONE

MONDAYS, since she had been secretary to Tony Welsh, were not the joy they had been when she had been secretary to his predecessor, Mr Neale, Jolene fretted as she drove herself to work that morning.

When she had started work at Templeton's she had felt that she really did have her feet on the ladder-rungs of a first-class career. But things had changed. She still enjoyed the work she did, but it was not the same. She knew why it was not the same, too. Mr Neale had been a gentleman; Tony Welsh most definitely was not. Of course, Tony was much younger, but that was no excuse...

Jolene parked her car in the firm's car park and wished that Mr Neale had not had that slightly adverse medical report which had made him decide to retire early. She had only been working for him for three months when he had left.

She entered the plush Templeton building, reflecting that she had only worked for Tony Welsh for three months too, though it had not taken her longer than a week to know that Tony was the worst sort of office wolf—the insidious kind.

Never did he say a word out of place or a word which could be construed by anyone else as any more than a mere compliment to herself. Yet never did he miss an opportunity to ogle her, to brush closely by her or to touch her in some 'accidental' way.

5

In the interests of office harmony she had often bitten back some sharp remark along the lines of his keeping his hands to himself, although on Friday she had come close to letting go.

Jolene approached her office door recalling clearly how he had bent over her to explain some point about the work in front of her. There had been no need at all for him to place a seemingly casual arm about her shoulders while he explained, but he had. If he could not tell from the cold way she had shrugged his arm from her that she did not want him to paw her about, Jolene thought as she opened her office door that Monday, the day was drawing near when she would let him know so—verbally, and bluntly. Married men—huh!

'Ah, Jolene!' Tony beamed at her when she went in. 'I trust you haven't done anything this weekend that I wouldn't do.'

Her insides screwed up on the instant. But again she bit back some acid comment. 'Good morning,' she managed civilly and, making some cool comment about how she'd spent the weekend trying to do something in the garden now that winter seemed to be over, she went to her desk, complimenting herself on her control.

She was not complimenting herself on her control half an hour later, however, for within the next thirty minutes a couple of things happened which were to leave her feeling disbelieving—and angry—and vocal.

To start with, Tony Welsh had chosen to give her a hand-written piece of work which she simply could not decipher. She stopped typing and looked up, to find that he was watching her from his desk in his own office.

'Having trouble with my writing?' he enquired smilingly, and, before she could leave her seat to take the work to him, he had left his desk and was over at her desk, all ready to translate it for her.

I'm getting paranoid, she calmed herself when, since she had had no trouble in reading his handwriting before, the idea came to her that he had made his writing indecipherable on purpose.

'It's quite simple, Jolene,' he began, but as he bent over her—her cold treatment of him on Friday apparently being water off a duck's back—his arm once more came about her shoulders.

Nauseated when she could have sworn that his hand actually squeezed her shoulder, she knew then, office harmony or no, that she was going to have to say something or explode.

'Will you kindly...' she began through gritted teeth, when suddenly the door opened and a pretty young woman came in.

Immediately Tony took his arm from about her shoulders, though not before the woman visitor had spotted what Jolene realised must have seemed, if not exactly an embrace, then a welcome familiarity. The moment had evaporated when Jolene could have given voice to her feelings, though. But on noticing that the woman wore a top coat as protection from the crisp March weather, she realised that she could not, therefore, work in the building. It was then that—since Tony was apparently struck dumb—her loyalty to the company's image forced her to be the one to deal pleasantly with this member of the public who appeared to have wandered up to the second floor by mistake.

'Can I help you?' she enquired, and was ready to redirect her—only to be utterly astonished when the woman shrilled at her,

'You can help me by leaving my husband alone!'

Jolene was still looking at her in amazement when Tony suddenly ceased to be dumbstruck, and exclaimed sharply, 'Roz! For heaven's sake!'

'For heaven's sake nothing!' the pretty brunette shrieked hysterically. 'You've done nothing but sing "Jolene's" praises since you were promoted to this job, and I know damn well you're having an affair with her...'

'An affair?' Jolene suddenly came to, unable to credit that it was *her* the woman was talking about. 'I assure you...'

'I don't want your assurances! I've had enough of those from him!' the woman snapped. '"I'm working late again tonight, darling!"' she mimicked.

'We do work late sometimes!' Tony told her. 'Now this has gone far enough, Rosalind,' he blusteringly tried to take charge.

'It's gone *too* far!' his wife cut him off, and went into an exaggerated tirade of how she had caught them about to cling to each other passionately when she had come in.

'If you'll leave us, Jolene, I'll sort this out,' Tony again tried to take charge. But his wife appeared to have simmered silently for too long, and she was too overwrought to let him get another word in. And, while Jolene was more inclined to stay to convince her how totally mistaken she was, rather than to leave, Rosalind Welsh went ranting on.

Finding that she was unable to get a word in either, however, Jolene was forced to hear the woman out, while at the same time she could not but wonder what kind of loathsome husband Tony was, that he should provoke his wife into this state.

'If you'll only listen...' she tried to get in again, only to realise that there was no reasoning with the woman when, looking near to nervous exhaustion, Rosalind Welsh cut her off.

'I've listened *enough*!' she cried. 'Morning and night, and the weekends too, I've listened to him singing your praises, while by comparison I'm told that I'm a useless wife and mother. Well, I've had it with him,' she said, 'I'm divorcing him—and—I'm naming you! I'm...'

'Naming me?' Jolene echoed incredulously.

'I know you fancy him!' the demented woman cried. At that point Jolene knew that, aside from there being no reasoning with her, Rosalind Welsh was never going to know peace of mind about her husband. Not while she was his secretary, at any rate.

Feeling angry with Tony, and deeply sorry for his wife, Jolene decided that this whole sordid scene had gone on far too long.

'Believe me, Mrs Welsh,' she said, surprising the woman into silence by going to collect her jacket and shoulder-bag, 'I wouldn't fancy your husband if he was first boiled and then disinfected.' With that, while they both gaped at her, she walked out of her office, and out of her job.

By the time she had reached the car park, Jolene had gone from being angry, through being furious with Tony, to being outraged by all that had taken place, and then just plain sickened by the whole nauseating scene.

Seating herself behind the steering wheel, she inserted her key in the ignition, then paused. Would she have felt so furious or so sickened had she not had that terrifying experience with a married man all those years ago? She had thought she was long since over it, but...

Her hand fell back into her lap, and suddenly her thoughts had gone to six years ago when she was sixteen and keen to have a Saturday job.

She was an only child, so that probably accounted for the way she had always been a little over-protected by her parents. At any rate, it had taken a great deal of discussion and a great deal of persuasion on her part before her parents had finally agreed that she could take the shop job she had found for herself.

The job had not lasted long, though. For she had quickly learned that not all men were as nice as her father.

She had felt disgusted, degraded and frightened when the married owner of the small shop had cornered her in the back room just after they had closed for the day. Never would she forget the dreadful lusting look that had come over his face when the man who outwardly appeared an impeccable pillar of society had told her in vulgar, explicit terms that he had always had a fancy for a virgin.

With her face draining of colour, Jolene had stared at him, not quite believing what she was hearing from this man whom her father himself had personally vetted before allowing her to work there.

'You've grown into a raving beauty,' the licentious shop owner had gone on, and while, frozen and as though turned to stone, Jolene had stared at him, he stated, 'You must be dying to know what it's like.' As he started to come nearer, he ended greedily, 'I'm just the man to help you find out.'

He had reached her and was standing in front of her blocking her way when Jolene, transfixed with fright and only half comprehending, suddenly snapped out of her trance.

This was here and now and, for the first time in her life, her parents weren't there to help her. But she was past thinking rationally what she should do, and she reacted on instinct alone. The nearest thing to hand happened to be a small wooden-backed brush that more usually partnered the dustpan.

Reacting blindly, she grabbed up the brush and hit him and hit him and hit him with it. She saw his hands go up to his head when she caught him a heavy blow near his ear, and heard him roar. Though whether he roared from anger or pain, she did not stop to find out. For, still acting on instinct, she pushed violently past him and ran out of the shop, and did not stop running until she reached the gate of her home.

She had never gone back. Nor had she told her parents why she had finished her Saturday job. They had just accepted that she had got the urge to try a Saturday job out of her system, and never knew the trauma that had struck that Saturday in particular, and which had darkened her Saturdays, and other days, for a long time to follow.

Shortly afterwards she left school and started secretarial college. By the time she had completed her studies, she had recovered and was no longer afraid or anxious when left alone in the same room with any man.

By that time, though, when one or two of her friends were already thinking of getting married and settling down, she was thinking of making a career for herself in big business. As top student in her class, she had a feeling for office procedures, and thought she had quite a lot to offer an employer.

Initially, though, she had problems on two counts. One: that there were no 'big business' type of firms in her part of Somerset. The other: that no prospective employer seemed to take her stated desire for a career seriously.

'Are you sure it's a career in an office you want?' one of them had asked. 'With that face and figure, you could take the lot on as a model.'

'Good afternoon,' Jolene had told him politely, and had left the man staring after her dumbfounded—she had not the smallest wish to work for any man who didn't put her excellent qualifications before her shape, her blonde hair and green eyes.

Eventually, however, she did find one such. But after working for kindly Mr Gabriel for two years, Jolene, with her capabilities in no way stretched, knew that if she was going to realise her full potential then she was going to have to move on.

That chance came unexpectedly and out of the blue when a short time later her grandmother died and left her her small bungalow in the village of Priors Aston, in Essex.

Jolene, on her tri-monthly visits to her grandmother's home, had always liked Priors Aston. Indeed, she felt at home there herself. But it was only after her grandmother had died, and after she had come to terms with the sadness of that fact, that on the last of the subsequent 'attending to matters' trips to Priors Aston Jolene started to think she might quite like to live there permanently.

'The bungalow will be no trouble to sell.' Her father was addressing her mother as the two of them decided what was best to be done with their daughter's inheritance. 'We can put the money in the building society for Jo-Jo, and when . . .'

'Actually, Dad,' Jolene found her voice—and nerve, since she had an idea that she was about to hurt her doting parents—'I was—er—well, actually, I shouldn't mind at all living here.'

It was done, said. Startled at this never-thought-of notion, both her parents had stared at her, open-mouthed. Her mother was the first to recover.

'You want to leave home?' she asked, looking totally scandalised.

There followed a month where the subject of Jolene's leaving home was put under the microscope. 'You'll have to give up working for Mr Gabriel,' was one point raised by her father.

'I know,' Jolene had replied quietly.

'It's not cheap, running a home,' was a point her mother mentioned.

'I know,' Jolene had agreed.

Though it was when her father smiled and told her mother that he thought they should make her an allowance to help pay for such things as the rates and the maintenance of her bungalow that Jolene knew, with some relief, that they were getting used to, and accepting, the idea that she would soon be leaving them.

'I don't want you to give me an allowance, Dad,' she had told him then, and, addressing both her parents, 'I'd—er—like to stand on my own two feet if I can.'

Fourteen months after she had said these words, Jolene faced the fact that she was having a struggle making ends meet. She had left her home in Somerset a year ago, and had found herself a more exacting job than the one she'd had with Mr Gabriel. She was doing very well in her job, too, but, having recently had to find an unprepared-for amount for some extensive rewiring to her property, she sat back to review the situation. Without question, she had only to ask and her parents would help her out like a shot. But, having gained her independence, she did not want that. And so, since it appeared that nothing was certain where property was concerned, and that for all she knew the central heating, or the plumbing, or anything else, might be the next unprepared-for catastrophe for her earnings, it seemed to her that she had better do something about finding a job that paid more.

She found that job—with its much higher salary—in Chelmsford, in the head offices of Templeton's, manufacturers of heavy machinery for the home and export market. Templeton's had large works and some offices in Hampshire and they paid well. Having started work in the Chelmsford offices, Jolene worked hard and reckoned that she earned every penny she received. But she had no complaints, because for the first time she felt stimulated, using all her office skills and learning fresh ones. She began to enjoy every moment of it—and then Mr Neale had retired.

Jolene came out of her reverie with a start to realise that she was still sitting in her car in Templeton's car park. Rushing back into her mind came the ugly scene which she had just been embroiled in. She felt less furious than she had, but the scene had left an unpleasant taste in her mouth.

Again she reached forward to turn the ignition key, and then suddenly she began to get cross. Why should she leave a firm that paid so well? She needed that salary, and she was fully prepared to work hard for her rewards. It was not as if she had done anything wrong, for goodness' sake! It was not her fault that Templeton's had engaged a man on their management side who was such a creep.

For five minutes more Jolene sat in her car, torn between the pride that would have seen her thumbing her nose at Templeton's and driving home to Priors Aston—and reason, that said that if some other calamity happened to her property then she would probably have to sell her home to pay for it.

Pride might well have won the day, however, had she not, when reaching for the ignition key a third time, recalled how one of the other secretaries who had had a personality clash with her particular boss had asked for and got a transfer to another section without any trouble.

When Jolene thought of how she had worked at Templeton's for six months and yet still did not know half the people who worked at that vast establishment, she got out of her car, and headed for the personnel department. If luck was with her, she could stay on at Templeton's, and might not ever see Tony Welsh again.

'But why do you want to move from your present section?' Miss Caldicott asked, glancing down at Jolene's file which she had extracted from a cabinet drawer. 'I thought you were getting on so well there.'

'I—was,' Jolene replied, and realised, without knowing why, that she seemed to feel more loyalty to Rosalind Welsh than her creep of a husband in that she could not divulge any of what had taken place that morning. Though the way the poor woman was shrieking her head off, it would be a miracle if someone had not overheard what was going on. 'Our personalities clash,' she drew out of the hat, though since she did not like

Tony Welsh as a person she supposed that wasn't too far from the truth.

But Miss Caldicott was shaking her head. 'I haven't a secretarial vacancy anywhere I can place you at the moment,' she said apologetically. 'I'm sorry,' she added as she leafed again through her file. 'Your references from previous employers are excellent, and aside from speaking highly of you, Mr Neale put in a special recommendation about you before he left, but...' She broke off. 'Couldn't you go back and try again? I'm sure Mr Welsh...'

'I couldn't,' Jolene interrupted her, and guessed, when she saw Miss Caldicott appear to study the application form she had completed over six months ago, that in reality the woman must be searching for some kind way in which to tell her that it was Mr Welsh or nothing.

Realising that she had as good as said that already, Jolene wished she had saved her pride and had driven straight out of the car park. She got to her feet, intending to spare Miss Caldicott the trouble of finding more tact, when she saw that the personnel officer seemed to be suddenly arrested by something on her application form.

In the next instant the birdlike woman was darting a look at her, and was bidding her a quick, 'If you'd like to wait, I won't be long.' And, so saying, Miss Caldicott had left her desk and was making for the door marked 'Chief Personnel Administrator'.

Jolene had been watching the door that had closed after Miss Caldicott for a few minutes on and off when her attention was again drawn to it as it opened. This time, however, Miss Caldicott left the door open as she smiled, stood to one side and, placing a hand on the door-panel, said, 'Mr Raven will see you now.'

Jolene had been mystified as to why the woman should have taken her file in to the high-up administrator, but she was doubly mystified as to why he should agree to see her. The way she saw it, if Miss Caldicott knew that there were no secretarial vacancies, then she could not see how Mr Raven, purely by virtue of being in a senior position, was going to conjure one up. But, since she was there, and since she had nothing else to do with her time that morning, she returned Miss Caldicott's smile and went into Mr Raven's office.

'Good morning, Miss Draper,' he stood from his desk to greet her affably, and as Miss Caldicott closed the door on them he invited, 'Take a seat.' He then took his own chair. 'Miss Caldicott tells me you're having problems getting on with Mr Welsh,' he opened.

Wondering what she had started, and although she did not seriously consider that Tony Welsh would come out of this other than smelling of roses, Jolene did not see how she could blacken his name when he had a wife and children to support. What could she say anyhow? Tony had never said a word which, when repeated, would not sound totally innocent. His brushing against her, his touching her at every opportunity, would be scoffed at too as no more than accidental contact.

'He . . .' she began. 'His . . .' she amended, and still felt too sick inside to want to tell anyone about Rosalind Welsh's visit that morning, and all that had taken place. 'His ways aren't Mr Neale's ways,' she managed lamely.

'But you've always been so adaptable. I've a progress report here after your trial period which states how very adaptable and quick and eager to learn Mr Neale found you.'

What could she do? What could she say? While she felt warmed that Mr Neale had obviously said nice things about her, she still wanted to shut that morning's happenings away in a dark corner.

'I'd—rather work for someone else, other than Mr Welsh,' was what she did say, and, knowing that with or without Rosalind Welsh's visit it would have probably come to this anyway, Jolene began to think that she was wasting not only her own time but Mr Raven's too, since clearly he could not do any better than Miss Caldicott in finding her a vacancy.

Then suddenly, while she was preparing to get to her feet yet again, she was aware of Mr Raven giving her a very severe scrutiny.

'What are you like in the "confidentiality" department?' he enquired solemnly.

'As close as the grave,' Jolene assured him, changing her mind about getting up and leaving when she saw that Mr Raven was not the sort of man who asked questions purely for the fun of it.

Then, making her blink, he flipped a quick glance at her file, which was open in front of him, then remarked, 'I see that you speak Russian.'

To say that she was a little staggered was putting it mildly. She almost said 'Pardon?' But she had heard him perfectly plainly, and since he appeared to be quite serious she quickly got herself together, to recall that the application form which Templeton's had given her had insisted on knowing what academic certificates she had, regardless of whether she thought them relative or not.

'I've a small qualification in Russian,' she agreed, re-membering how she had taken Russian at school, had scraped through her exam with a pass, and had then dropped the language as a subject when she had started secretarial college. 'But there's not much call for Russian around here,' she said with a smile.

He smiled back, and almost threw her again when, 'Do you have a current passport, Miss Draper?' he wanted to know.

'Yes,' she replied. 'A ten-year one.'

Half an hour later, Jolene was driving out of the Templeton car park, scarcely able to believe her luck. Of course it might not happen, she steadied herself as she headed her car in the direction of Priors Aston, and it very probably would not happen, but—she had been put on standby to go to Russia!

Mr Raven had only been able to give her a sketchy outline, and of course it was all very confidential, but it seemed that a secretary, a Russian-speaking secretary, might well be needed to accompany someone of the higher echelon to Russia.

Jolene felt like singing, that a morning that had started so disastrously should have turned out the way it had. For if she wanted proof that her interview with Mr Raven had really taken place, she had it in the fact that he had sent her home to collect her passport. Apparently there was no time to be lost in applying for a visa for her, so once she had picked up the passport she had to go and have some photographs taken.

Jolene was still trying to hold down her excitement when, with both passport and photographs in her shoulder-bag, she later returned to the Templeton building.

Her instructions had been that she must deal with either Mr Raven or Miss Caldicott and none other, and it was Miss Caldicott who instructed her to sign her visa photographs and also her visa forms, then told her, 'I'll see to the rest of it. Now,' she said, and it was back to the mundane and the ordinary when she went on, 'Unfortunately, one of the secretaries in Purchasing has gone home with a back problem. We don't know yet how long she's going to be off sick, but could you go along and fill in for her?' Miss Caldicott was smiling again as she added, 'In the meantime, I'll keep my eyes open for something more permanent for you.'

Jolene worked happily for Gordon Hutton that first week. She could not in truth have said that her work in the purchasing department actually sent her into ecstasies, but if the work she did was just a shade on the dull side, then she was kept busy, and besides, she still had the inner glow of knowing that she might, she just might, be going to Russia.

She had always been selective over boyfriends, but if there was no one she fancied going out with then she had quite enough to do with keeping her bungalow and garden in good order. But when the second Friday since she had worked for Gordon Hutton came around, and still no word came from Miss Caldicott about the Russian trip, a lot of Jolene's inner glow began to fade. She had been so busy mugging up on her Russian that she had not been out in the evening for two weeks; not that she had wanted to, but that was not the point. The point was, was her nightly poring over Russian textbooks a complete waste of time?

When the following Monday rolled around, Jolene had spent the weekend doing some more swotting and telling herself that if she had not heard anything from Personnel by Wednesday, then she would go along and see Miss Caldicott to ask what was happening.

Wednesday came and went, however, without Jolene contacting the personnel department. For one thing, Mr Hutton seemed to have found her a backlog of work, which gave her very little time to do anything but the job in hand. And, for another, Jolene had reminded herself that it had never been definite that she would be called upon to go anyway, and that she had only been put on standby.

By the following Monday she had put away her Russian textbooks and had put out of her mind any idea of going to Russia. She parked her car and entered the Templeton building having made the decision that she would go and see Personnel, though. Not about Russia, she reckoned she could forget about that, but about the prospect of working somewhere else other than in Purchasing.

All thoughts of going to Personnel went from her head, however, when as she was turning into the corridor which led to her own office she saw Tony Welsh coming towards her.

She had not clapped eyes on him since she had walked out of her job as his secretary, and she felt then that the most she could manage in the way of civilities would be a curt nod as they passed. But she did not get far. For, 'Hello, Jolene,' he said warmly, and, while his eyes reassessed her proportions, 'I've missed you so much.'

'Really?' she replied coolly, and would have walked by him had he not come and planted himself squarely in front of her.

'Don't be like that,' he said, and to make her squirm, and to hold her there, he took hold of her arms. 'I couldn't help Roz coming in that day, but she won't do it again. Nor,' he added quickly, his hold on her tightening when she tried to break his grip, 'will she be divorcing me, as she said.'

'Will you let me go?' Jolene started to snap, then to her disgust, not to say alarm, she saw a lustful light coming into his eyes.

'Stone me, I fancy you!' he said in a thickening voice, and before she could stop him he had pushed her against the wall, and she was revolted to feel his vile wet mouth against hers.

Panicking wildly, she was ready to scream blue murder. But suddenly a harsh, cold, never-before-heard voice gritting, 'What the hell...?' broke through her panic, and as that voice registered with Tony Welsh too, he abruptly let her go. They both turned to stare at the tall, bronzed, extremely well-tailored, icy-eyed man who was looking at them both as if they had just crawled out of the woodwork. Jolene was still trying to recover when that harsh voice came again, and in no uncertain terms clipped, 'If the pair of you want to indulge in sex-play, get off the company's premises! You're paid to work here, not to come here to work off your carnal desires.'

Jolene was still in shock when the man, somewhere around his mid-thirties, she would have said, gave her and then Tony Welsh a contemptuous look, then strode off.

'Hell, it had to be him!' she heard Tony say, but she was suddenly over her panic. She was recovering fast too from her shock at being so spoken to by—whoever he was, for she had never seen him before—and she was all at once furious with both Tony Welsh and the superior-looking autocrat who had just strode off.

In fact, she felt furious with the whole male population just then as she hissed at Tony Welsh, 'You dare, ever dare to touch me again, or even lay so much as a finger on me, and I swear, by all I hold holy, that I'll take out a private summons against you for assault! Have you got *that*?' she snapped, and when she could see from his expression that he was now more taken aback than lustful, she went storming to her office.

She was angry on and off throughout that morning whenever she thought about the horrible incident. As well as Tony Welsh earning himself some of her ire, the immaculately suited male who had happened by came in for some of her wrath too. How dared he accuse her of indulging in sex-play? Who the blazes did he think he was?

By early afternoon, though still angry whenever she thought about it, Jolene had simmered down quite a lot. She was able to give Mr Hutton her usual smile at any rate when around two-thirty he called her into his office.

'I don't want you to take dictation,' he told her genially when he saw that she had brought her notepad with her. 'I've just taken a call from the top floor—Miss Frampton would like to see you.'

'Miss Frampton?' Jolene queried, the name, although vaguely familiar as though she had heard it since she had worked at Templeton's, otherwise not meaning anything to her. 'Who's Miss Frampton?' she asked.

Mr Hutton's eyes positively twinkled as he revealed, 'Only the very highly esteemed private and personal assistant of none other than Mr Cheyne Templeton, our chairman and head of company himself. Perhaps,' he hinted, 'it might be an idea if you went now.'

Jolene took his hint, along with his directions, and made her way to the top floor. She hardly dared to let herself get excited that this could be something to do with the Russian trip, lest, since that ghastly man this morning seemed to have some authority, she had been reported higher up and was now being summoned to be told off by Miss Frampton.

It couldn't be the latter, could it? Miss Frampton had better things to do, surely, she pondered as she found the door which Mr Hutton had directed her to. If it was, though—she began to bridle—then she would not stay working for Templeton's another minute.

Trying not to get cross before she started, Jolene knocked at the door and then entered the most sumptuous of offices, to be immediately disarmed when a pale-looking woman of about forty looked up and smiled.

'Jolene Draper?' she queried, leaving her desk and coming to shake her hand as she said, 'I'm Gillian Frampton. Come and take a seat.' Jolene was still taken with the effortless charm of the woman when, seated in a chair beside hers at the desk, Gillian Frampton asked, 'How's your Russian?'

'I'm going...' Jolene took a grip on the excitement that suddenly surged in her, to rephrase her question and ask, 'Am I going, then?'

The highly esteemed PA nodded. 'On Wednesday. I'll...'

'On Wednesday!' Jolene exclaimed. 'You mean—this Wednesday?'

'I'm sorry to spring it on you at such short notice,' Gillian Frampton apologised. 'And I take all the blame that Mr Raven couldn't tell you more. But, since I wasn't certain whether you would be required to go, I expressly asked him not to say too much. You can manage to be ready by Wednesday?' she asked.

'Oh, yes,' Jolene said eagerly, knowing that for a trip like this she could be ready by tomorrow if necessary.

'You'll be a great help to Mr Templeton, I feel sure. You'll...'

'Mr Templeton? Mr Cheyne Templeton? The head of...' Jolene broke off what she was saying as Mr Cheyne Templeton's private PA nodded, and started to smile.

'Come along,' she said, rising from her chair, 'I'll take you in to see him.'

Feeling more than a little winded that she, Jolene Draper, had been the one selected to go to Russia with the chairman of Templeton's, Jolene followed Gillian Frampton across the plush carpeting.

She swallowed nervously as the top-notch secretary in whose footsteps she had to stand for a short while popped her head around his door and asked, 'Is it convenient for you to see Jolene Draper?' Jolene reckoned that he must have nodded or made some sign that it was indeed convenient, for Gillian Frampton was pushing the door wider.

What his efficient PA said after that though, Jolene could not have said. For as, with a smile ready on her lips, she followed her into the room and looked at the man who had started to rise from the most enormous desk, she was shaken rigid by shock.

Any semblance of a smile abruptly departed as she recalled how on her way to the top floor she had wondered if the ghastly man who had that morning been so insulting had reported her to someone higher up. But, as she looked across the room to the tall, bronzed and extremely well-tailored man, Jolene knew that he had no need to report her to someone higher up. The reason for that being—that they did not come any higher up! For that ghastly man—the man who had mistakenly thought he had seen her responding to Tony Welsh's passionate embrace—was none other than the chairman of the company, Mr Cheyne Templeton.

Somehow, going to Russia had suddenly lost some of its appeal.

CHAPTER TWO

FOR how long she stared at Cheyne Templeton in shaken silence, and for how long he stared at her as though of the opinion that his PA must have taken leave of her senses if she thought he was going to take this woman with him anywhere—let alone Russia—Jolene had no idea. Suddenly, however, just as he seemed about to erupt, he switched his gaze from her to Gillian Frampton.

Jolene, since her experience of him was that he did not hesitate to say what he thought, anticipated that Gillian Frampton would soon be on the receiving end of something not very polite from him. Her glance followed his to where in some trick of this different light in his office his PA seemed to look more off-colour than merely pale. Then Jolene was staggered to hear his voice, gentle almost, as he quietly told his personal assistant, 'I'll take it from here, Gillian.'

'I'll see you later, Jolene,' Gillian Frampton smiled, and, clearly having missed the hate vibes that flashed between a pair of large green eyes and a pair of dark grey eyes, she left them to it.

It did not take long for the tone of voice Jolene had previously expected to enter the head of Templeton's voice. And she went more and more off the idea of boarding a plane with him on Wednesday when he snarled nastily, 'Ye gods, couldn't they get anyone else?'

It was touch and go at that precise moment that Jolene did not tell him what he could do with his job—and his

27

plane trip. But from somewhere, she knew not where, she managed to find sufficient control to hang in there and tell him, 'I consider that remark most uncalled-for! What you saw this morning was none of my fault. It...' she broke off, seeing from the glint in his eyes that he was not exactly thrilled that she was excusing her own behaviour by putting the blame on someone else. Again she came near to telling him what he could do with his job, but again she found some control. 'For your information, Mr Templeton,' she began bravely as she thought of all the hours she had spent just thinking about going to Russia and hoping that if she did a good job it might stand her in good stead should a senior secretary's job become vacant, 'I'm more career-minded than I'm man-minded. I'm good at my work too,' she drew a fresh breath to tell him.

'And have your eye to promotion, no doubt?' he queried before she could go on.

'I can't see anything wrong in that,' she replied stiffly. 'It's a woman's world today, as well as a man's.'

'When I want a lecture on the equality of the sexes, I'll ask for it,' he grunted, and, his manner dismissive, he commanded, 'Stand by to fly to Moscow on Wednesday.'

He had his phone in his hand and was already getting on with the next item on his work agenda before she had risen an inch from her chair. Jolene left his office not knowing whether she was glad or sorry that, by the look of it, she was going to act as his temporary—thanks to her knowledge of Russian—secretary.

'How did it go?' Gillian Frampton asked.

'I'm to stand by to fly to Moscow on Wednesday,' Jolene relayed, but could not refrain from asking as

Gillian again invited her to take a seat, 'Is he always so blunt?'

'Mr Templeton has only just returned from almost a month abroad on other business,' the other woman replied. 'Which means he's got only two days in which to clear up the pile of work which I couldn't handle for him in his absence.'

'You didn't go abroad with him, then?' asked Jolene, having assumed that his PA normally went with him on his outside assignments, but that the only reason she was not going on this assignment was that she had no knowledge of the Russian tongue.

'Oh, it's not necessary for a secretary to go with him every time he goes abroad,' Gillian told her. 'But with the Russian schedule looking extremely punishing to me—though you will get a break,' she inserted as though she was afraid of putting her off going, 'it will make for efficiency all round if Mr Templeton can have his impressions recorded on the spot and not be bogged down by the paperwork side of things. He thinks on his feet,' she confided, 'so you'll have your work cut out to keep up with him. But,' she smiled, 'I feel sure that you'll manage.'

Wishing that she felt half as confident, but that sort of talk being just the challenge her career-orientated self needed, Jolene put Cheyne Templeton's harsh manner out of her mind and, as excitement began to stir in her again, 'How long shall I be away?' she asked.

She drove home that night knowing that she would be away for about two and a half weeks. Her head was still buzzing with the information Gillian Frampton had given her during her briefing.

Jolene garaged her car, recalling that besides Moscow and Leningrad, Gillian had said her skills would be needed at a place called Irkutsk. She had never heard of it before, but with so much else to think about she decided to concentrate on being the best Russian-speaking substitute for Gillian Frampton that Templeton's could provide.

She realised as she prepared her meal that evening that she had some way to go before she could begin to be anywhere near as good a PA as the efficient Miss Frampton.

Indeed, Jolene had eaten her meal and was in the middle of doing her washing up when it suddenly came to her just exactly how efficiently, and well, Gillian Frampton worked for her employer. Because only then, she recalled firstly how Gillian had spoken to her only for a short while before taking her in to see the boss, and then how she had asked, 'How did it go?' and had learned that she had, by the sound of it, passed muster, had she revealed any of what the Russian trip was all about.

In fact, she had seemed so relaxed that it had taken until now to realise that the outcome could have been very different. Only now did Jolene see that had she not said what she had when she had come from Cheyne Templeton's office, Gillian Frampton would have smoothly, and with some tact, found a way to tell her that she would not after all be required to go.

Feeling a trifle peeved that had her face not fitted she would not be going, Jolene rebelled for all of two minutes. Who in creation did Templeton's think they were anyway? she mutinied. For about ten seconds of her two minutes her imagination took off to picture herself telling Cheyne Templeton personally tomorrow that she was afraid she could not make the Russian trip after all.

She dismissed that notion when her true self came to the fore, and she knew that since there surely could not be sufficient time now for a visa to be obtained for another secretary, it just was not in her to let anyone down.

Not that they'd have had any qualms about letting her down, she thought while the edge of mutiny was still on her. Of course, she suddenly realised, Gillian Frampton had not known that she and Cheyne Templeton had happened across each other earlier that day. So she would have no idea that her services in the 'let down gently' department would not be needed. As Jolene saw it, had expediency not won the day, Cheyne Templeton would not have thought twice about telling her himself that she could forget the Russian trip.

She spent the next hour wishing she was flying to Moscow on Wednesday with anyone but Cheyne Templeton. At the end of that hour, though, her chin was tilted at a stubborn angle as she vowed that she would make a success of this, the biggest challenge in her life. Then she went to the phone to ring her parents.

'You're going where?' her mother cried, panicking already at the thought of her baby travelling to Russia.

'I'm a big girl now, Mother,' Jolene laughed, and although she dearly loved her parents, she was able to see that, if she had not left home when she had, then her parents might, in their love for her, have stifled her and her need to live her own life. 'I couldn't be more excited about it,' she told her, and when later she replaced the phone she knew those words for the truth.

For excitement was back with her and, as she pushed thoughts of Cheyne Templeton from her, she could not wait for Wednesday.

Tuesday had to be got through first, however. After her interview with Mr Raven several weeks ago, and in anticipation, she had enquired of her bank how much notice they would need to get her some roubles, and had been informed that Russian currency could not be obtained outside the USSR. That being so, she went to her bank in her lunch hour that Tuesday and picked up some traveller's cheques. Next she tore round the shops and, completing last night's list of things she thought she might need to take with her, tore back to her office.

She had barely caught her breath, though, when Mr Hutton, his curiosity obviously straining at the leash, was calling her into his office and telling her, 'This is getting to be a habit, Jolene—your presence is again requested on the top floor.'

'I'd better go now, then,' she smiled, and went from his office, through her own office and out towards the lifts. But for the confidentiality of her new and temporary position, Jolene would have loved to have stayed and satisfied Mr Hutton's curiosity. But that was just pride, and she knew it. For, when she got around to thinking about it, she was enormously proud that she was going to Russia with the industrialist Mr Cheyne Templeton, to explore the possibility of a joint engineering project.

Initially, however, Jolene was to doubt that she would be going anywhere with Cheyne Templeton. She had thought she had been summoned to the top floor for a last-minute briefing from Gillian Frampton, but a decidedly peaky-looking Gillian told her, 'Mr Templeton would like to see you, Jolene. Would you like to go through?'

'Close the door,' Cheyne Templeton ordered curtly when, after first tapping on it, Jolene went in.

'You wanted to see me,' she said, observing in one glance that he had not overnight turned into a man she would, unpaid, leave home for.

Unspeaking, he pointed to the chair where she had sat yesterday. Unspeaking, Jolene went over to it. 'There's a lot riding on these initial interviews in Russia,' he began without preamble as soon as she was seated.

'I assumed that might be so,' she said quietly, having worked out for herself that to make it worth anyone's while the project they were going to discuss just had to be worth millions—not to mention its value on the employment of manpower side.

'Then I can rely on you to behave yourself should I take you?'

His 'should I take you' was not lost on her, but initially, Jolene was more indignant over what else he had said than upset that there still seemed to be some doubt that she was going.

'Behave myself?' she exclaimed, her lovely green eyes starting to emit sparks. She didn't have to take this from anyone, and that included him.

'You know quite well what I mean!' Cheyne Templeton rapped. 'I'm not having these talks put in jeopardy purely because of some man-mad . . .'

'Man-mad!' Jolene erupted. 'If you're referring to the way Tony Welsh backed me against a wall yesterday, then I've already told you it was none of my fault. If you'd care to check with Personnel,' she went fuming on, heedless that yesterday she had gained the impression that this man did not care to have her put the blame on someone else, 'then I'm sure they'll have it down on file that I . . . I . . .' she started to flounder, '. . . that I don't—couldn't—get on with Tony Welsh and that I asked for a transfer.'

'You seemed to be getting on with him all right when I came across the pair of you,' he retorted sharply. And before she could get another word in, 'Did you suppose, Miss Draper, that after seeing you—for the second time—yesterday, I wouldn't check you out?'

'If you've checked me out then you know. . .'

'It seems strange to me,' he cut in toughly, 'that your personality clash with Welsh should become suddenly too much for you and that you should apply for a transfer *only* on the day that his wife should come to the office to ask you to leave him alone.'

'It wasn't like *that*!' Jolene protested, her horror showing that, by the sound of it, it must be all over Templeton's that she and Tony Welsh had been having some sort of sordid affair. A sordid affair which had only ceased when his wife had come to the office and shrieked her head off about it. 'I couldn't stand him or his sneaky amorous overtures. I enjoyed my work before he came,' she charged on, too angry at being falsely accused to tell it other than the way it was, "but when Tony Welsh's wife called that day and it became evident that she would never know peace of mind, not while I was his secretary anyhow, I walked out.'

She had come to a heated end, but as she stared into cold dark grey eyes she knew that this man was quite prepared to go on this important trip without a Russian-speaking secretary if he did not get the right answers.

'If there's any truth in what you've just said, why keep it hidden from Personnel?' he charged. 'If it's as you say and Welsh is the sickening type of office Romeo you describe, then don't you think Personnel should know of it?'

'I couldn't prove anything,' Jolene was forced to confess. 'Up until yesterday when he openly made a grab for me, he was, as I told you, sneaky with it. Besides,' she went on, 'I didn't know he was going home night after night singing my praises until his wife cracked—not that I blame her,' she added. 'Anyhow, as I said, I liked the work I was doing until he came. I was good at it too,' she asserted. 'I . . .'

'Oh, I know you're good at your work,' Cheyne Templeton surprised her by chipping in.

'You do?' she exclaimed.

'Confound it, woman!' he said sharply. 'Leaving aside that there's a question mark over your penchant for married men, do you think Raven in Personnel would have recommended you if you weren't already earmarked as being the right PA calibre?'

Jolene's reaction on hearing him suggest that she had a penchant for married men was an angry one. But her ire was at once neutralised when she heard what else he said. By the sound of it, she had been earmarked for a PA slot at some later date—which just had to mean advancement within the company. Didn't it?

'I was down for promotion?' she just had to ask.

Sternly, Cheyne Templeton studied her eager face. Then, his mind at that moment made up, apparently, 'If you're that set on a career, you'd better go and arrange with Miss Frampton to draw some expenses,' he told her. He was already on the next task in hand as, realising that he had just as good as agreed to take her to Russia with him, Jolene vacated her chair.

She floated out of his office on air. Many emotions had visited her during the short time she had been with him, but the emotion uppermost in her as she went into Gillian Frampton's office was happiness.

She did not question why she should feel so happy to know that she was going to a foreign land with her alien employer. Though had she paused to question it, she would have been able to answer quite easily that the reason why she was so happy was that to have notched up a business trip with no less a person than the chairman himself must surely increase her promotion prospects further.

'Mr Templeton said I'm to arrange with you about some expenses,' she smiled at Gillian Frampton when she walked by her desk.

The PA smiled, giving no hint that she might well have been equally ready to deal with the matter had Jolene left Cheyne Templeton's office to tell her that she was not now required to fly to Moscow tomorrow.

Shortly after that Jolene left the top floor and descended in the lift, wondering if there was anything at all which the superb PA had not thought of. Because, as well as arranging her expenses, and arranging for a company car to be at Priors Aston at the crack of dawn ready to deposit her at Heathrow for eight o'clock, Gillian Frampton, having told her that Mr Templeton would have her passport, visa and flight ticket with him, had handed over the very latest in portable typewriters.

'It'll save you chasing round to hire one,' she had smiled. And in answer to Jolene's question as to whether it was all right for her to tell Mr Hutton that he would not be seeing anything of her for a few weeks, Gillian had said, 'Of course. Although since I imagine Mr Templeton will consider he owes Mr Hutton the courtesy of telling him that himself, I shouldn't be surprised if he doesn't already know.'

The proof that Cheyne Templeton had already been on the phone to him was there for Jolene when she had barely got back to her desk and Mr Hutton came from his office. 'Well, this is a real feather in your cap, Jolene,' he beamed, quite clearly puffed up with pride that his secretary, albeit only on loan while his other secretary was off sick, had been chosen to accompany the chairman.

'I'm sorry I couldn't tell you about it before,' she apologised. 'But...' She discovered she did not have to add any more.

'I quite understand,' he told her, and after a few more minutes of seeming as if he thought it was a feather in *his* cap too, he came down to earth to realise that since she would not be in tomorrow, they had better get on with some work.

Jolene was later than usual getting home that night, and after an evening spent in packing, taking a long telephone call from her parents and checking that her home was neat and tidy to return to, it had gone midnight when she finally got to her bed. She was up very early on Wednesday morning and, although bathed and dressed, she was still finding last-minute jobs to do when a uniformed chauffeur rang the doorbell of her bungalow.

Excitement was high in her as the chauffeur, who had introduced himself as Frank, carried her large suitcase out to the limousine standing at the kerb, and she followed hanging on to the portable typewriter which the efficient Gillian Frampton had given her yesterday.

They had been driving for about twenty minutes, however, when the chauffeur turned off the main road and explained that he had another passenger to pick up.

'Mr Templeton?' Jolene guessed, having begun to wonder if she was likely to see him again before Moscow.

'Mr Templeton doesn't live locally,' Frank replied. And, leaving her to decide that Cheyne Templeton would either be driven to the airport by someone else, or that he would drive himself and leave his car in the long-term car park, he went on, 'First I've to pick up Mr Edwards, and then Mr Shaw.'

Hiding her surprise that by the look of it, unless they were just giving Mr Edwards and Mr Shaw a lift somewhere, it seemed likely that they would be four on the flight to Moscow on Templeton business, Jolene sat back to await developments.

Before another twenty minutes had passed, however, she had become acquainted with both Alec Edwards and Keith Shaw. Alec Edwards, who wore glasses, was balding and seemed to be the studious type; he was somewhere in his mid-forties, Jolene thought. Keith Shaw, though, seemed little more than thirty, and was the friendly type. Both men, it appeared, were very well qualified engineers. Alec, Jolene quickly learned—and all before they reached the airport—worked on the production management side, while Keith worked on the technical 'nuts and bolts' side, specialising, so he said, in doing the impossible.

'How about you?' Keith Shaw questioned. 'I refuse to believe that with a face like that you're an engineer too!'

'I'm a secretary,' she replied. Keith's manner, as opposed to Tony Welsh's, was so open that she was in no way offended. 'I—er—speak a little Russian,' she said modestly, only mentioning it in case they were wondering what she was doing on this trip in place of Cheyne Templeton's PA—if they knew her.

'Don't we all!' Alec Edwards put in pleasantly, if not very enthusiastically.

'You both speak Russian?' she queried.

'Mr Templeton insisted that we both did an intensive crash course—with a slant on engineering terms—before we could come,' Keith Shaw replied.

'Only some,' Alec Edwards chipped in, 'did better at it than others.'

'Genius will out,' Keith owned with no attempt to look bashful, and as the three of them burst out laughing, Jolene knew that she liked these engineering men and that all augured well for personalities to blend comfortably on the trip.

Some while later she was thinking that maybe she had been a little previous with that opinion. Either that or she had forgotten, if not Cheyne Templeton, then the way in which he could so quickly make her angry. For she, Keith and Alec were at the airport when Keith again said something to make her laugh. Merriment was still curving her lovely mouth when suddenly she became aware of Cheyne Templeton joining them.

She saw his glance flick to her mouth, but when he otherwise looked icily through her, all signs of happy humour went from her face, and she saw no reason at all why she should afford him a smiling greeting.

Not that, apart from the briefest of nods in her direction, he had any greeting for her whatsoever, but having uttered a greeting to the two engineers he was asking amiably, 'Your wives not here to see you off?'

Swine! Jolene fumed, knowing full well that not only was Cheyne Templeton telling her that both the engineers were married, so 'hands off', but she had a nasty suspicion that he would be watching her throughout the entire two and a half weeks too!

Fuming inwardly, she felt like telling him she knew jolly well that both Keith Shaw and Alec Edwards had wives—had she not seen them taking a fond farewell of their wives and families when the limousine had called at their homes? She did not say anything of the kind, however, but when a general move was made to go and check in, and Keith and Alec suddenly got mixed up with the crowd, she just could not resist the pleasant question, 'Isn't your wife here to see you off?'

Her eyes were innocent and large when, looking at her sharply, Cheyne Templeton replied curtly, 'I'm not married.'

'Some female's had a lucky escape!' Jolene muttered to herself, only to discover from the narrowing of his eyes that the man she was going to have to work closely with for the next two and a half weeks had the acutest hearing.

To her gratitude, she had little to do with him during the flight. And at the end of the flight, excitement had her in its grip again, and it did not matter to her so much as it had that it seemed he was going to watch every move she made. Because she was here on her first overseas assignment, and surely anyone aspiring to be a top-notch PA would have to be a real stick-in-the-mud not to get excited about that!

She was still feeling excited when, having just been handed her passport by her employer, she stood before the uniformed young man at Passport Control and felt hard put to it not to beam a smile at him when he scrutinised her features for what seemed an age. Then, having returned her passport to Cheyne Templeton for hotel formalities, she was collecting her luggage from the conveyor belt prior to having it X-rayed *out* of the airport.

She had a brief tussle with Keith when he insisted on carrying both her luggage and his own, and then the four of them were outside the airport and on the pavement. And her excitement took off again. For here she was in the USSR, where, besides Moscow and Leningrad, a place called Irkutsk would start to mean something.

CHAPTER THREE

By SATURDAY evening a good deal of Jolene's excitement and enthusiasm had evaporated. So OK, she had expected to work hard, but there was work—and then there was *work*! While she admitted that Cheyne Templeton had not spared himself either, he had kept her nose glued to the grindstone near enough from the very first thing on Thursday morning.

No, before that, she corrected herself. For they had arrived at their hotel in Gorky Street at a little after six on the Wednesday evening, and while she had stepped forward to the receptionist, keen and eager to try out her Russian, she had discovered that the receptionist spoke better English than she herself spoke Russian.

Their room keys, plus small paper slips which would permit them past the hotel's doorman each time they came in from the outside, were handed out, and they took the lift. Keith and Alec were on a different floor and they got out first, saying that they would see the others at dinner.

Engrossed to see a female floor attendant seated behind a desk when she and Cheyne Templeton got out at their floor, Jolene was absorbing the atmosphere when he told her curtly, 'This is your room,' and as he moved away to his door along the corridor, 'We'll dine at eight. Don't be late!'

42

'Wouldn't dream of it,' she replied guilessly, and went into her room to unpack a few of her belongings and to investigate the plumbing.

Dinner was a three-course meal which began with fish and red cabbage, and was followed by what Keith decided 'had to be reindeer'. The meal ended with a piece of iced shortbread.

'If that's it, I think I'll take me a look round Red Square,' commented Keith.

'I've had sufficient,' Alec said, getting to his feet. 'I'll come with you,' he added.

'Would you like to come with us, Jolene?' Keith, as she had hoped he would, asked her.

Eager to take in all and everything, she was about to accept the offer with alacrity when Cheyne Templeton cut in. 'I'm afraid I need to brief Jolene on a few matters.'

'Some other time, then,' smiled Alec, and while Jolene was getting over her surprise that for once, if not directly, her employer had used her first name, the two engineers went on their way. After that, there did not seem to be any time for her to do any sightseeing.

Indeed, she mused, she might just as well have left her camera at home, for she had barely been outside the hotel for anything other than business. She had only just found time to visit the bank around the corner.

'You won't need too many roubles,' Cheyne Templeton had told her when on Thursday morning she mentioned that she would really like to get some Russian currency before she went much further.

'I won't?' she questioned.

He shook his head. 'Foreign currency is welcomed here. It's quite legal, and easier, to spend sterling,' he added, but he accepted that she still wanted to change a traveller's cheque for some roubles and even told her where the bank was, then waited while she crunched her way across through the snow to find it.

No sooner was she back in the hotel, though, than the serious business they were there to do started. It began with a warm-up visit to a factory and from then on meeting after meeting where afterwards Cheyne Templeton gave her dictation after dictation—all to be typed back before her head hit the pillow at night. He worked fast and furiously, and Jolene could only be glad that everyone they had so far met spoke English, and seemed determined to practise it at every opportunity. If she began to wilt under the strain so that sometimes she found even her own shorthand indecipherable, then she would remember from having been there what the subject was all about.

So far she had been able to fill in the few blanks accurately. She thought, too, that she was getting used to the pace at which Cheyne Templeton worked. Though if she could do no other than admire his hundred per cent dedication to the job in hand, not to mention that he never forgot a thing and seemed to have a photographic memory for detail, then she still thought he was something of a swine in his attitude towards her. Even when she barely had a minute to herself, it seemed to her that he was still watching her every move.

She got ready for dinner that Saturday evening feeling sure that she would not be called upon to work flat out again tomorrow. Surely the chairman of Templeton's rested sometimes! Please let it be tomorrow, she offered up a prayer. She had not done a scrap of sightseeing as yet—surely Sunday was just the day to see Moscow?

Because it was warm in the hotel, Jolene wore a two-piece suit of lightweight wool. She left her room with her thoughts on how she had come across a section of the hotel selling picture postcards and how she had sent her parents a card with a picture of the Moscow Metro showing its marbled halls. Her hopes were high as she secured the door of her room that maybe tomorrow she would have the chance of travelling on the Moscow Metro—when suddenly she espied Cheyne Templeton leaving his room some way up the corridor.

Wishing she had timed it better, for she had no particular wish to see him before she had to, Jolene realised that it would be childish not to wait for him. The way one always had to wait for the lifts at mealtimes, it went without saying that she'd have to wait with him at the lifts anyway.

'Have you finished that report I gave you after lunch?' he asked, his eyes flicking over her beautifully proportioned features and neat shape in her red two-piece, as he joined her and she fell into step with him.

Biting down hard on the 'Give me a chance!' that sprang to her lips, Jolene halted by the lift and murmured politely, 'I thought—rather than keep everyone waiting for dinner—that I'd save some of that report in case I get bored for something to do later this evening.'

'I've noticed about you, Miss Draper, a certain impudence you would do well to check,' Cheyne Templeton told her crisply.

Immediately she made her face a blank. But as the lift arrived and she glanced at him before she got in, she could not help noticing that for all his crisp tone, and for all she was 'Miss Draper' this evening, there seemed to be a very definite upward quirk to the corner of his mouth. It was almost, she thought as the lift began to descend, as if he was having a hard time not to laugh. As if her politely spoken if sarcastically meant comment had amused him!

Alec Edwards and Keith Shaw were already at the dinner table when they joined them. But as Jolene got busy with her egg, caviare and beetroot salad starter, she quickly learned that she would not have time to visit the Moscow Metro tomorrow. Not because she would be working, though, but because tomorrow they would be leaving Moscow.

'We're leaving Moscow?' she exclaimed.

'I thought you knew we had a meeting in Irkutsk on Monday?' her employer replied.

Yes, she did know, he had mentioned that meeting only that afternoon, but she had thought that Irkutsk must be a suburb of Moscow or something. Somewhere at any rate where they could get there and back quite easily by taxi.

'I—hadn't realised that we'd have to change hotels, or to leave Moscow in order to be in time for the meeting,' she said, trying not to notice that Keith seemed to be trying not to laugh, while Alec was observing his caviare as if in some fascination. 'What time are we leaving here?' she questioned, perhaps with some vague notion of maybe still getting in a visit to the famed Metro.

'Our plane takes off just after...'

'Plane!' Jolene exclaimed. Somehow it had never crossed her mind that she would be taking to the skies again before her return trip back to England. 'We have to fly to get there?' she queried, thinking that if she had had five minutes to spare since she had learned that she would be visiting Irkutsk, she would somehow have mugged up where, in relation to Moscow, it was to be found.

'Since our meeting is most definitely arranged for this coming Monday, to go by plane seems the only way to travel if we're to keep our appointment,' Cheyne Templeton said drily, and while by that time Jolene was starting to get the general idea that Irkutsk was quite some way away, his voice had taken on a pleasant note as he let fall, 'I'm reliably informed that even by plane it will take us all of seven hours to get there.'

'Seven hours!' she exclaimed, aware that one could almost go from England to America in the same amount of time. 'Where the dickens are we going?' she just had to question.

Her jaw nearly hit the table when, blandly, Cheyne Templeton told her, 'Siberia—didn't you know?'

'*Siberia!*' she croaked. And, as she got herself together, 'You're—joking?' she suggested, mindful that Keith and Alec were smirking their silly heads off.

'You'll learn, Jolene,' the man to whom she was earlier 'Miss Draper' began 'that I never joke about business.'

She was still trying to surface from hearing that tomorrow she would be flying to Siberia when Keith remarked, 'Don't say you didn't bring your thermals!'

'I did, actually,' she told him coolly, and tucked into her meal, grateful that simply because she had always thought of Russia as a cold place, she had thought to pack some woollen undergarments.

They left Moscow from a different airport from the one they had arrived at, and by courtesy of Aeroflot. The plane they boarded was a TY154, and had very few seats vacant, Jolene noted. They took off just after midday to the accompaniment of pop music, and the music was still coming through the speakers well after they were airborne. She forgot about the pop music, though, when a stewardess diverted her attention by bringing round small terracotta-coloured bowls of mineral water. Wanting to cram every experience she could into this working expedition, Jolene drank her water and, looking at the man in the seat next to her, she saw that Cheyne Templeton too had quenched his thirst.

Some time later lunch was served, and three hours after they had taken off from Moscow they landed in Omsk, to disembark while the aircraft was refuelled.

As they walked from the plane to the transit lounge, though, Jolene was all at once very much aware of her employer; of his height and the air of authority which he just exuded.

'Coffee?' he queried generally when, having climbed the steps to the transit area, the two engineers had found a table.

Wondering why on earth she should suddenly have felt so aware of Cheyne Templeton, Jolene took the opportunity of his going to order coffee to give herself a mental shake. For goodness' sake, what in creation was the matter with her?

'I wonder what the time is?' Alec pondered aloud, and gave Jolene something else to think about.

'It's just gone half past three,' she consulted her watch to tell him.

'That's what my watch says too,' Alec smiled. 'But since there are about ten time zones in the USSR, I reckon we must have crossed a couple of them already.'

'Oh,' she murmured, only then starting to get to grips with how vast the USSR really was.

They remained in Omsk for about an hour, and whatever the time in Omsk then was, and her watch still said half past four Moscow time, dusk was falling when everybody made a move to return to the plane.

Jolene found that she was again walking side by side with her employer when, negotiating the icy steps of the transit building prior to going to the aircraft, she suddenly felt his hand firm on her elbow. For no reason her heart leapt a beat and then steadied when at the bottom of the steps he let go his hold on her. With no need then to keep her eyes on her feet and where she was putting them, she raised her head and, all at once, as she looked at the skyline, she was held spellbound by the most magnificent sunset.

With the sun a big round beautiful ball in the sky, she was so enraptured that she just had to share it. 'Look...' she began, as with her eyes alive in her face she turned to Cheyne Templeton. But suddenly, as she looked up into his dark grey eyes, she forgot completely what she had been going to say. For as he looked solemnly down into her upturned face, she was all at once breathless—and she had the craziest notion that so too was he.

That crazy notion did not last above a second, for to prove that he was not in the slightest breathless he was curtly telling her, 'You'd be better employed in looking where you're going, Miss Draper.'

So what if there was some hard-packed snow about? she thought belligerently, and to show him that she was as firm-footed as he no matter where she looked, she swiftly put some space between them.

Jolene spent the time until she boarded the aircraft in being certain that her imagination had been playing her tricks and that she had not felt in any way breathless either. All such thinking went out of her head, however, when as she made her way down the aisle to the seat she had previously occupied, she saw that it was now occupied by Keith. She smiled at him as she went past him. If he wanted the window seat, he could have it. He could have Cheyne Templeton to go with it, too, she thought a shade mutinously and, seeing that Alec was seated not too far away, she went and sat next to him.

She knew that Cheyne knew where she was sitting when, as he came down the plane to his seat, his eyes registered where she was. Just counting his sheep, she thought sourly, but could not help but wonder, when she cared not a button, why she should suddenly feel so belligerent about him.

'Hope you don't mind changing seats with Keith,' Alec said, giving her a fatherly smile. 'Only Mr Templeton wanted to go into some complicated engineering problem with him and, as you know, he never likes to waste a minute.'

Jolene gave him some 'didn't mind a bit' answer, but she did not feel very talkative, and spent the next half-hour realising that Keith had not taken her seat in the aircraft because he wanted a window seat, but because Cheyne Templeton had ordered him to sit there.

She had by then discovered that her employer was something of an engineer himself, so it was quite feasible that he wanted to spend the next three hours discussing some engineering problems with Keith. But she doubted it. As well as discovering that the head of Templeton's was a qualified engineer, she had also discovered that he worked on the principle of never leaving until tomorrow what he could do today. That being so, she was very near a hundred per cent certain that if he

wanted an engineering discussion with Keith he would
have conducted it in the first three hours of their flight,
and would not have so much as considered leaving it
until the second half of their flight.

Not that it bothered her in the slightest that he clearly
did not want her sitting next to him. For goodness'
sake—as she fleetingly recalled Tony Welsh's way of
going on—far from being piqued, it was a welcome relief
to have a boss who was not trying to get as close as he
could to her the whole time!

She was lifted out of her sole topic of thought when
the stewardesses again brought little dishes of water
around. *'Spahsseebah,'* Jolene thanked her, and heard
Alec trying out his Russian too.

But when they had downed the mineral water, it was
as though Alec had primed his vocal cords, for he was
in a talkative mood from then on, telling her about his
wife, and his wife's job at the local health centre, and
about his children, now fully grown. 'It's funny,' he said,
'but every time I go away on this sort of trip, I spend
weeks looking forward to it, and then, no sooner am I
away from home than all I can think about is getting
back to it again. Crackers, isn't it?' he ended.

'It's not crackers at all,' Jolene told him warmly. 'It
just means that your home and family mean a lot to
you. Which,' she smiled, 'is how it should be.'

They chatted on after that until there was a sort of
tea break where they were served a cake, a small tub of
jam, and a packet of coffee powder. Not quite sure what
she was supposed to do with the jam, Jolene watched
to see what the Russian travellers did with it. Though
when she saw that they ate the jam with a spoon, and
ate the cake afterwards, she decided that she preferred

her jam spread over her cake. She had just demolished it when cups of hot water came round.

She added the coffee powder to it, as did Alec, and, his vocal cords primed once more, when he learned that she had quite a big garden to look after they had a lengthy discussion on gardening.

The plane had started to descend at Irkutsk when he said, 'Oh, by the way, I discovered that Irkutsk is five hours ahead of Moscow. Which means that we are now eight hours in front of the UK. Which also means,' he added, pushing back his cuff prior to adjusting his watch, 'that the time is now a quarter past midnight, Irkutsk time.'

Jolene had altered her watch too, and she stayed close to Alec as they landed and boarded one of the two small airport coaches that came out to the tarmac to ferry passengers to the airport building. She stayed near to the fatherly man again when half an hour later they collected their luggage.

It took the taxi about fifteen minutes to convey them to their hotel, but no sooner had the documentation side of things been dealt with and room keys handed out than Keith was making noises, since he had missed his dinner, about finding something to eat.

Feeling not at all hungry, Jolene, with her watch now reading half past one in the morning, was more inclined to the idea of getting herself settled in her room. She was surprised, therefore, when Cheyne Templeton, who up until then had seemed barely to notice that she was there at all, suddenly addressed her.

'How about you, Jolene?' he enquired. 'Are you hungry?'

Masking her surprise that apparently no member of the Templeton firm was to be allowed to go to bed hungry, she replied politely, 'No, I'm not, actually.'

'Then get to bed,' he commanded her curtly. 'We have a full day tomorrow.'

Cheyne Templeton, Jolene considered, had the most aggravating knack of rubbing her up the wrong way! But, 'Goodnight,' she managed, her pleasant 'Goodnight' extending to cover both Alec and Keith. Then, having hidden that she was starting to get irked by her employer's bossy attitude, for all he was boss, she headed for the lifts and for her room.

She did not sleep well in the narrow bed provided, but she was mollified somewhat when she thought that if she was having trouble, if the size of her bed was hotel regulation size, then the tall, broad-shouldered Cheyne Templeton must be finding getting to sleep a nightmare!

She had had enough of trying to get to sleep by six o'clock, and although dawn had not broken and it was still dark outside, she got up and bathed and dressed.

Daylight had broken at seven o'clock, and at half past seven a knock on her door revealed a woebegone-looking Keith extending his wrist, saying, 'Are you going to go all Women's Lib on me if I tell you that a button has come off the cuff of this brand new shirt, and that I'm prepared to let you have my next Aeroflot tub of jam if only you'll sew it on for me?'

What could she do? She laughed. 'I presume you haven't brought a sewing kit with you,' she tried to sound severe as she invited him in.

'You've got a TV in your room—we haven't in ours,' Keith commented as he held his arm still while she stitched the button back for him. 'That's great,' he said a minute later as she broke off the cotton. 'Are you coming to breakfast?'

Pausing only to pick up her bag and her room key, Jolene followed him out of her room—then stopped as though frozen. For waiting by the lift, and looking down the hall at them, stood Cheyne Templeton, and it was clear from the thunderous expression on his face that he had put his own interpretation on why she and Keith Shaw were leaving her room together before breakfast that Monday morning.

Turning to check that her door was secured, Jolene, observing that Keith was still fiddling about with his cuff, determined that she was not going to make any excuses. She had not forgotten that Cheyne Templeton believed she had a penchant for married men, but, as stubbornness set in, she reminded herself that she was totally innocent, Keith Shaw's coming to her room was totally innocent, and she'd be blowed if she would explain. And, as her stubbornness set solid, Jolene decided that her too-quick-to-jump-to-conclusions employer could jolly well believe what he liked!

Her chin was tilted at a defiant angle and there was a light of battle in her eyes as she walked with Keith to the lift. Then, as Cheyne looked blackly from her to Keith, and looked as though he was about to sort the pair of them out, Keith, about the sunniest person she had ever met, was saying, 'Good morning, sir. In the interests of looking immaculate for this morning's meeting, I've just borrowed your secretary to sew a button back on to my shirt.'

Knowing full well what Cheyne had been thinking, and might still be thinking, for all she knew, Jolene refused to say good morning to him. Not that he looked ready to break out into spots about that, she observed when, with his expression not much lighter, the three of them stepped into the lift.

'Alec went down earlier,' Keith filled in what was a cold silence as the lift descended. 'But these beds—did you . . .' he broke off as the lift stopped and several more people got in.

The lift emptied at the second floor as everyone went to find a breakfast table. Alec was sitting in solitary splendour at a table for four, and they went to join him.

Jolene saw him look at Keith's shirt cuff, and after the 'good mornings' were out of the way he said 'I told Keith that you'd be bound to have brought your needle and thread,' and smiled.

By then Jolene had lost some of her stubbornness, and supposed it was no bad thing to have Alec confirm for Cheyne Templeton that Keith had only been in her room for the purpose he had stated.

'I don't suppose you can sew either,' she commented to Alec, but her glance had flicked to Cheyne, and as she stared at him she rather got the impression that he had realised that, while she would willingly sew a button on for Alec, he, her 'dear employer', could lose every one of the buttons off his shirt, but he'd be wasting his time in coming to her room to ask her to sew them back on again for him.

Breakfast consisted of a large cup of delicious buttermilk-type yoghurt, followed by slices of cheese and slices of the tenderest beef together with dark brown bread and a dish of butter. There was also a cheesecake type of confection which was very tasty too, and a dish of jam. Suddenly hungry, Jolene set to with a will, and drank coffee while she decided to give the tea a try

tomorrow, as Alec, who seemed to have the capacity for
finding out all sorts of irrelevant bits and pieces, told
them that it was twenty degrees below freezing outside.

If things were freezing outside, however, then as the
morning progressed a thaw started to set in with Jolene.
Perhaps the fact that Cheyne himself seemed to have
forgotten to be curt with her had something to do with
it. But in any event she no longer felt antagonistic to
him as they made their way to the large factory where
it seemed they were to spend most of the day.

Anticipating that it would be here in Irkutsk that her
Russian would be put to the test, Jolene realised that it
was too late now to wish she had done the crash course
which had included Russian engineering terms.

But as a delegation stood in the reception area and
she prepared to perform what introductions were necessary, she was little short of dumbfounded when Cheyne
Templeton, having previously met the Director of
Engineering, it seemed, stepped forward and shook
hands with a greying, smartly suited man somewhere in
his early fifties.

'*Dobrahyee ootrah*, Anatoly,' she heard him say, and
while she quickly decided that to say 'Good morning'
in Russian was probably the only Russian her sharp employer knew, he went on to dumbfound her some more
when, asking fluently after the Director of Engineering's health, he set about introducing his team.

'*Ehtah Gahspahzhah* Jolene Draper,' he turned first
to her. And while she shook hands with the Director,
and as Cheyne introduced his two engineers, there began
a round of introductions with the Russian engineering
team.

'I am most pleased to meet you,' said a man of about thirty, who was introduced to her as Viktor Sekirkin, and who smiled warmly at her and, as he gripped her right hand, insisted on speaking English.

A moment later they were shown to a cloakroom where in the general hubbub of shedding their warm coats, hats, scarves and gloves, Jolene exchanged smiles with Ivetta Shvetsova, a woman of about forty who was Alec's counterpart in engineering.

Sociably they all went off to drink coffee, and although there was another woman by the name of Tatiana who was standing by to interpret, her services were not called upon.

Shortly afterwards they embarked on a tour of the massive factory, with Jolene and Tatiana trailing in the rear. Tatiana, Jolene rather thought, was trying to look as interested as she was trying to look whenever they stopped, which seemed to be every two minutes, to stand and stare for interminably long periods by some large hunk of machinery or other.

Jolene, stifling a yawn, was still trying to look as though her work began and ended with a lump of green-painted oily-looking metal when she saw Cheyne Templeton flick a glance at her. Immediately she tried to appear as though she was riveted by the intricacies of the piece of machinery. She could not, however, resist a quick look to him as she sensed his glance move away from her. To her amazement, though, when if anything she would have thought he would be frowning at his perception that she was finding it tough going to maintain a show of interest, Jolene saw that he was in the act of suppressing a definite upward curve to the corner of his mouth.

Certain that he had just won a battle against allowing himself a smile, she wondered had she again—unwittingly—amused him?

Whether she had amused him or not, though, she afterwards felt much more friendly towards him than she had. The tour of the factory was completed by lunchtime and they were entertained to lunch by the Director and his engineers. As they went to their places, however, Jolene found herself walking with Cheyne Templeton for a few moments and, rather than allow him to say something in any way acid about her short-comings on the morning's tour, should he be so inclined, she hurried in to say brightly, 'I'd no idea you could speak Russian!'

Very much aware of his glance down at her from his lofty height, she anticipated an arrogant reply along the lines of 'What makes you think you know everything?' But, to show that he was not a snarling brute the whole of the time, his tone was quite pleasant when he disclaimed, 'It's only a smattering picked up from a cassette on my drive to and from the office just recently.'

A smattering! she thought, having heard him speaking quite fluently to Anatoly Markov in Russian. And, as she remembered how up until recently he had been out of England on other business, and realised that his knowledge of the Russian language must have been picked up in a very few days, she just could not resist saying, 'You must live hundreds of miles from the office, then.'

She was then fairly shattered on two accounts—the one, that she discovered that she was quite interested to know where he lived, the other, that as Cheyne Templeton looked down at her, he actually smiled a most super smile, as he queried, 'Am I to take that as a compliment?'

She was glad to be saved from an answer when at that moment he was diverted to go and sit next to the Director at the large luncheon table, while she was urged by Viktor Sekirkin to come and sit next to him.

'You enjoyed your visit to the factory?' asked Viktor as they began their meal with thick smoked salmon accompanied by green olives.

'Very much,' she told him, a lie not only permissible but definitely required in the circumstances, she felt. To her relief, however, Viktor, as he asked her to call him, had no intention of spending his lunchtime filling in the large gaps in her education about engineering machinery, but filled in a few of the blanks on her education about Irkutsk.

During her first course she learned that Irkutsk was the administrative and economic capital of Siberia. 'Siberia, as you know, I think,' he smiled, 'means sleeping land.'

Their next course was bortsch, a soup of which the main ingredient was beetroot. Viktor was most attentive to her as he first served her from the soup tureen and then helped himself.

Jolene was half-way through her soup when she glanced around the table to observe that Ivetta Shvetsova was deep in engineering conversation with Alec Edwards, while Keith and Tatiana were politely conversing. When her glance fell on Cheyne Templeton, however, Jolene just knew that although he appeared to be giving the Director his entire concentration he was at the same time every bit aware of what each of them was doing.

They were on their third course, which was beef Stroganoff, rice and carrots, when as Viktor suggested, 'Maybe you would like a guide to show you Irkutsk?' Jolene happened to glance again at the man sitting next to the Director.

It was then that she began to doubt that she had ever seen anything on his face that could be termed a smile, let alone a super smile. For Cheyne had his glance fixed on no one but her, and as his dark eyes glinted dangerously, and his expression—with not a smile in sight—looked little short of threatening, Jolene was remembering his accusation that she was man-mad, and how he had told her that he was not having the Russian talks put in jeopardy because of it.

'I'm—er—not sure quite what free time I'll have,' she replied as tactfully as she could to Viktor, and was back to hating Cheyne Templeton again. It could have been that Viktor was offering his services as a guide, or was offering to get her a guide, but suddenly she felt too stilted to be natural with him. Fair enough, with Cheyne Templeton close enough to eavesdrop on her conversation, he could well have overheard Viktor's suggestion, and could—knowing her employer—well have thought that she was leading Viktor on. But dammit, they were here to do business; was she not supposed to give Viktor the time of day?

Jolene tucked into her final and fourth course of mousse and ice cream and endeavoured to appear as if there was not so much as a trace of mutiny in her.

After coffee, they took a small amount of exercise when they visited the factory's photographic exhibition. But the whole time she was studying the photographs of the end product of the factory's labours, she was rebelling against having this trip of a lifetime spoilt by the man she was there to work for.

Guessing that she would never come this way to work again, Jolene gave the meeting all her attention when later they adjourned to sit round a table, when both sides talked 'possibilities and feasibilities'.

The meeting went on for some good while, and then it was time to leave. The Director and the engineers, with Tatiana still in tow, escorted them to where they had left their top coats and accessories.

The Director and Cheyne Templeton were still in conversation as they walked towards the outside door. Then everyone was shaking hands, and Viktor, to Jolene's exasperation when Cheyne was but a yard away, was saying, 'Perhaps you can find out if you have free time tonight. You can telephone to me and I can come for you at your hotel if...'

'I'm afraid my secretary has to work this evening,' Cheyne, not giving her the chance to reply for herself, cut in smoothly. Any pride Jolene might have experienced to hear him call her his secretary, though, was immediately negated the moment she looked beyond his bland expression to read an expression in his eyes that again warned her to behave herself. She said her goodbyes and stepped into the waiting car.

She was still feeling insurgent when back at the hotel she went to her room, changed, and fumed that, but for Alec and Keith, she would not go down to dinner.

Purely because she knew that she would not have Cheyne I'm-keeping-my-eye-on-you Templeton as her sole dinner companion, she did go down to dinner, though. She need not have been concerned about being called upon to enter into a friendly foursome, however, because, engineering being what they were about, it was engineering, and what they had seen that day, that ruled the conversation at the dinner table.

After dinner both Keith and Alec said that they were going to try to hunt up a beer in the hotel, which left Jolene, since they were again housed on the same floor as each other, to share the lift upwards with the man she was still not liking any better.

They were stepping out of the lift when, having been determined not to say a word to him, but having not forgotten that he wanted her to work that night, she suddenly found herself saying, 'Your place or mine?'

She had to give him full marks for instant comprehension. 'Bring your pad to the lounge area on this floor,' he answered shortly. 'We'll work there.'

CHAPTER FOUR

JOLENE awoke on Tuesday morning, saw that it was daylight and immediately wanted to go back to sleep again. In her opinion Cheyne Templeton was just too much!

For some moments she lay there, staring unseeing at the folded blanket which was inserted through an aperture in a sheeting bag, and which served as a kind of duvet. The man was tireless, was her considered opinion as, realising that if she was serious about a career then she should be welcoming this chance to prove herself, she pushed back the duvet and got out of bed. She thanked him not that his parting words last night had been, 'You needn't type it back tonight.' Superwoman she was not!

Her thoughts flitted to Gillian Frampton, the nearest she had seen to Superwoman, as she went into the bathroom and began to run her bath. It was something to strive for, she supposed, to one day be as superefficient as that charming and unflappable lady.

Fleetingly she wondered if Gillian Frampton liked her employer. She'd have to like him, wouldn't she? Jolene had no idea how long Gillian Frampton had been PA to Cheyne Templeton, but surely one would have to like the slave-driver to work for him.

Remembering that her employer had also mentioned that they would be breakfasting later this morning than they had yesterday, Jolene slowed her pace and wallowed in her bath as she pondered, still, did Gillian Frampton like him, and indeed, how could anyone like the impossible man?

She was towelling herself dry when the thought suddenly struck her, did *he* like anyone? Did he, in fact, like Gillian Frampton? All at once Jolene was recalling, quite clearly, that first day she had met him and how his tone when he had spoken to Gillian had been vastly different from the tone he had used when he had spoken to her. His tone of speaking to Gillian, she remembered without effort, had been quiet, even gentle!

A small frown wrinkled her usually smooth brow and from being in not so much of a hurry that morning, she was suddenly in very much of a rush. Swiftly getting dressed, she quickly brushed her hair and applied the small amount of make-up she wore, as if all the time trying to escape from something she did not want to know. Eventually, however, she slowed down and, letting her thoughts carry on to their natural conclusion, she just could not stop the question—was Cheyne being such a brute to her in particular because he had not wanted anyone but Gillian with him on this trip and was missing her? Was he, in fact, having an affair with his PA?

Feeling decidedly out of sorts at what her probings had brought her, Jolene left her room trying to tell herself that she was being ridiculous. She knew precisely why he was being a brute to her, for heaven's sake—he thought she was man-mad, and he was just out to ensure that her 'man-mad' tendencies did not put a spanner in the works of this business opportunity.

In any case, she assessed as she stepped into the lift, if Cheyne Templeton had been having an affair with Gillian Frampton, and had wanted her with him on this trip, then without a doubt he would have made darned sure that Gillian had gone on the same intensive crash course in Russian that Alec and Keith had attended.

Anyway, Jolene decided, as she left the lift and headed for the hotel's restaurant, he needed Gillian back in London, where she could be of immense help to him in fielding any problems that arose at that end. What did she care anyhow? Jolene discarded the issue as she neared the table that had been assigned to them. Cheyne Templeton could have as many affairs as he liked, it was nothing to do with her—she did not give a light!

Having taken a seat at the table where last night the four of them had dined, Jolene was surprised that, for all they were starting work later than yesterday, she was the first one down.

A minute or so later, though, the tall and attractive being in the shape of the man she loved to hate came striding easily through the restaurant doors. 'Good morning,' he greeted her civilly, and dropping his serviette over his lap and ignoring the yoghurt he reached for the cheese and dark brown bread. 'Not hungry?' he paused to enquire as, before he had tasted a morsel, he observed that she was neither sipping her yoghurt nor tucking into the bread and cheese.

'I thought I'd wait for Alec and Keith,' she replied.

'I shouldn't,' he remarked drily, 'they breakfasted an hour ago.'

'An hour... But I thought we were all starting later this morning?'

'Not Edwards and Shaw,' he replied. 'By now they should be hard at it doing the job which they're more especially here to do.'

'Oh,' Jolene murmured, but, quickly getting over her surprise, 'We'll be going to the factory later?' she enquired, and got an even bigger surprise when, expecting him to tell her at what time they would be leaving for the factory, he instead told her,

'We won't be going to the factory. You and I, in fact, won't even be in Irkutsk in a few hours' time.'

'We won't?' she echoed, her eyes large on his as she wondered where they were going now.

'There comes a time, Miss Draper, when man must rest,' he drawled. 'Listvyanka, I'm reliably informed, is the very place in which to recharge one's batteries.'

In Jolene's view, Cheyne Templeton's batteries never needed topping up! She had never seen any sign of them running down anyhow. But, just as she had never heard of Irkutsk before, this Listvyanka fell into the same category, and since she, Alec, Keith and their employer had travelled everywhere together since leaving London, it seemed no more than a normal question when she began, 'What time do we pick Keith and...'

'Forget married men for a time!' Cheyne Templeton cut in sharply, and when she stared angrily at him that just the mention of Keith's name on her lips should bring to the fore this man's belief that she had a penchant for married men, he was telling her abruptly, 'We're leaving both engineers here, you'll have to manage without them!'

Furious enough to want to throw her yoghurt over him, Jolene somehow managed to restrain the impulse to take some physical action against him. There was no doubting that she was inwardly on the boil, however, when, recalling his 'man must rest' remark, and feeling sorely in need of a rest—from him—she said through stiff lips, 'This Listvyanka—do I get a break too?'

Her boiling fury very nearly spilled over when he had the unmitigated gall to bark, 'Have you typed back those notes I gave you?'

Keeping her hands firmly away from her cup of yoghurt, not sure that she would not be decorating him with it yet, she snapped, 'You know I haven't!'

'Then you'll need your typewriter,' he rapped.

For about three tense icy seconds Jolene glared at him, and he stared furiously at her. Then, when all the odds were against it, they were suddenly both laughing. Somehow when they seemed poles apart, all at once her sense of humour came out, met his, and matched.

She was not laughing when three-quarters of an hour later she was back in her room, collecting her things together. For the suspicions which had earlier sprung to her mind were there in her head again, and were being added to. Because it was when she was recalling how a short while ago Cheyne Templeton had told her to pack her case as they would be checking out of the hotel that she also remembered something which Alec Edwards had told her. If memory served, it was on the plane to Irkutsk that he had referred to how, although things were becoming much more relaxed in the USSR, one could not yet move around freely. Alec had told her, she was certain, that one must still apply in advance to visit the locations one wanted to visit.

Jolene packed her belongings in a very solemn frame of mind, for suddenly it was very clear to her that when Cheyne Templeton had decided to go to this place Listvyanka without his engineers, he had envisaged taking a different female with him from her. At that moment Jolene knew that, since Gillian Frampton had intimated that she did sometimes travel with her boss, the London office could quite well manage without her, and that she had originally been down for this trip too— but something had happened to make her back out.

Convinced that Gillian had been scheduled for this assignment, Jolene realised that while Cheyne Templeton must have been out of England for a good deal of the time that his PA was making the Russian travel arrangements, he must have agreed these arrangements in advance. Since he would have had to sign his Russian visa application before he had gone away on his other trip, this man, who never flagged and who never seemed to tire, must have known and fully approved that he and Gillian Frampton would be leaving the two engineers in Irkutsk while they went to Listvyanka for a 'rest'.

Hating herself for her suspicions that Gillian Frampton was more to Cheyne Templeton than just his superbly efficient PA, Jolene tried to tell herself that it was nothing to her what sort of a relationship he had with Gillian anyway. Once more she assured herself that she didn't give a light whether he was having an affair with his PA or not. But as she closed her suitcase on the last of her packing and fastened it up, she could not help but remember that the gentleness in his tone when he had been speaking to Gillian Frampton had never been in evidence when he was speaking to her.

The time was nearing eleven o'clock when, with their luggage in the boot, Jolene sat beside Cheyne Templeton in the taxi which was to take them to Listvyanka.

Snow lay everywhere, and the temperature was way below freezing, but the sun shone brightly as they headed out of Irkutsk. Jolene still felt in a solemn mood, however, and she was glad her employer was not minded to entertain her with polite chat. Not that she could ever recall a time when he had put himself out to entertain her, or to indulge in chat for the pure politeness of it, she thought glumly, then instantly brought herself up short. What did she want, for goodness' sake?

She was unable to find the answer to that, but, knowing only that she suddenly felt more restless than she had ever done in her life, she looked at the snow-cleared road in front. Then she looked at the sides of the roads which were deep in snow. And all at once, as she looked at the sleeping land and at the for the most part leafless trees that seemed like tall poles on a white carpet, she began to know a sense of peace. The nearer they got to their destination of Listvyanka, the more that feeling of peace increased.

'It's incredible!' the whispered words slipped from her, as the taxi took them through the *taiga*—the forests that extended through countless miles between tundra and steppe.

'I couldn't agree more,' the man by her side said quietly, and most unexpectedly, and as Jolene turned to him she was taken by a tremendous feeling of being at one with him.

For the most part the trees that lined their route were giant pines interspersed with giant silver birch, but there were cedar trees too, and some larch, Jolene noticed. Then all at once, when everything around had been frozen and still, they came to a spot where flowing water met rock-solid ice.

'Can we stop?' Jolene could not prevent the exclamation, and warmed to Cheyne when, not taking exception to her request to do something not on his schedule, he straight away instructed their driver to pull over.

No sooner had the taxi halted than Jolene knew she could never be content just to sit and admire the scene from the motor vehicle.

Without another word she got out, and felt a sudden gladness in her heart when, as she stood by a rail at the water's edge, Cheyne came and joined her.

'This, I think, just has to be the river Angara,' he commented.

'Why *has* to be?' she queried.

'Because,' he obliged, 'I've a vague recollection of reading somewhere that while Lake Baikal has over three hundred rivers and streams flowing into it, it has only one outlet. That outlet's the river Angara—whose source, apparently, never freezes over.'

A little open-mouthed, Jolene stared from the running water to the forested hills and snowy rocks on the other side. Then her glance went to her left where a ship of some sort was making its way across the river near to where, in almost a straight line, free-flowing water met rock-solid ice that went on for miles and miles. Staring at this phenomenon in awe, she had all the proof she wanted that the ice was indeed rock-solid when, in astonishing contrast to the ship on water, she saw there in the distance that a lorry was travelling over the ice.

'That's Lake Baikal?' she asked Cheyne as she pointed to the frozen lake.

'That's it,' he replied. 'The deepest freshwater lake in the world.'

'Do you know how long it is?' she wanted to know.

'You make me glad that my reading's as wide as it's varied,' he smiled, and told her, 'Near enough four hundred miles, if I remember correctly.'

Jolene was certain he had a perfect memory, but, feeling in harmony with him for once, she smiled back and, very much impressed by the frozen lake, just had to gaze at it some more.

Then Cheyne was escorting her back to the taxi, telling her, 'You'll have plenty of time to look your fill later.'

'We're coming back this way?' she enquired.

He did not answer that question, but to her delight he told her, 'This is Listvyanka. My information is that our hotel's situated less than six hundred yards from the lake.'

Which it proved to be. Although any absurd thought that might have struck her that she and her employer were perhaps at the beginning of a more harmonious association was doomed within ten minutes of their booking into the hotel.

The hotel was much smaller than any they had so far used, being only three storeys high. Once their luggage had been brought to their floor, Cheyne dismissed the porter. Then he opened the door in front of them and stood back for Jolene to go in.

Stepping through the open door, she realised as he followed her in that he had come to check for himself her accommodation in this smaller hotel. Then surprise took her, because as she walked along a hall she observed that to one side lay a curtained bedroom and that to the other side lay a sitting-room. She had, in fact, been allocated a suite!

'Have you a suite too?' she enquired impulsively, and realised immediately that that was a daft question, because of course he would have.

His reply, however, made her stare at him in astonishment, when he told her coolly, 'We'll share this one.'

'We'll do nothing of the kind!' she snapped immediately, her eyes wide on his. Though as, rocking back on his heels, he stared back at her as though he thought she had just taken leave of her senses, Jolene felt she must have made the most appalling blunder. 'You do have a room of your own?' she then felt compelled to query.

Siberia had nothing on the coldness or the cutting quality of his tone when, the ice forming in his eyes too, he clipped, 'Don't flatter yourself, Miss Draper, I merely meant that, since this suite has a dining table for you to work from, it would be better to set up office in here.' With that he dropped her suitcase to the floor and strode to the door. 'We'll lunch in half an hour. See that you're punctual!'

When was she ever late? Jolene fumed as he closed the door decisively after him. Let him go hang, was her next furious thought, she'd be damned if she would go down to lunch—she'd starve rather!

Five minutes later she had calmed down a little, but was still angry at being spoken to in that way by him. 'Don't flatter yourself, Miss Draper,' he'd said. Who the hell did he think he was anyway? She was not the least little bit interested in him, for heaven's sake.

Another five minutes went by, during which Jolene was not at all sure how she felt about him coming and going as he pleased to her office-apartment.

After a further five minutes, though, she was starting to realise that the reason why she had so quickly jumped to the conclusion she had when he had stated, 'We'll share this one,' had been because of the suspicion she nursed that Gillian Frampton had been scheduled to come on this trip originally, and the suspicion that the two of them were having an affair. What more natural, if her suspicions were correct, with neither of the engineers around to tell tales when they returned to England, that Gillian and that brute Cheyne Templeton should share the same suite for anything but *office purposes*?

Jolene was stumped to know where that left her suspicions, however, when, with ten minutes to go before lunch, she questioned why then had Gillian Frampton booked him a separate room.

She gave up trying to get to the bottom of it when she went to the bathroom and washed her hands and tidied her hair, and was stung all over again when Cheyne Templeton's 'Don't flatter yourself, Miss Draper,' came into her head yet again.

Three minutes later she left the suite to go looking for the restaurant. She still felt angry enough to prefer to starve rather than eat with the swine. But—and here pride played a major part—she was determined, following that 'Don't flatter yourself' to show him just how *un*-interested in him she was.

She did not get much chance, however. For a start, she *was* late going in to lunch, though she hardly considered that it was her fault that it took her all of five minutes to locate the hotel's dining-room.

As dining-rooms went, it was a very nice dining-room, but she had never expected to have to negotiate four flights of steps down into the basement to find it.

'I'm sorry I'm late,' she offered aloofly, and, when it had cost her a very great effort to talk to Cheyne at all, she could have hit him when he ignored her.

Never, she thought as she tucked daintily into her first course of thinly sliced cold pork, smoked salty salmon and lettuce and cucumber salad, had any one man of her acquaintance so brought out the worst in her!

Never, she fumed as she drank a home-made tomato soup that was 'interesting' for what else it contained, had any one man made her feel so violent towards him.

She remembered the incident with the shopkeeper in her Saturday job six years ago while she ate her way through her next course of fish in batter. The violence that had been in her then had been brought on as a result of her terror, she reflected, and realised only then that that foul man would probably have caved in instantly had she thought to tell him not to be so stupid and that she would tell his wife.

But she had been too frightened to so much as think clearly that Saturday, she recalled, as she ended her meal with a piece of fruit cake and a cup of tea. She was thinking of Cheyne Templeton again and of how it was not terror or fear of him that made her feel violent towards him on quite a few occasions, when she became aware that he had finished his meal and that any second now—quite probably without having said a word to her—he would be leaving the dining-room.

Without a word to him, Jolene chose that moment to pick up her bag. She got to her feet and bestowed on the waiter who had served them a smile of such loveliness that he stared after her when, in the next instant, and with her head in the air, she left the dining-room.

Nor did she wait for the lift. With no wish to spoil her exit should the lift delay its arrival and give Cheyne time to join her, she made for the stairs.

She returned to her room, of the opinion that if Cheyne Templeton wanted her for anything, then he knew where 'the office' was!

She did not, however, see him at all that afternoon. She had plenty of work to be getting on with, though, and spent a good many hours at her typewriter, where every now and then she would break off to wonder why it was, in fact, that Cheyne Templeton of all men should make her react so intemperately. What was it about him, that he had the power to rile her so? It was so unlike the person she knew herself to be that, when she was not wanting to empty a cup of yoghurt over his head, she should be wanting to hit him.

When Jolene got round to thinking of her sense of humour and his sense of humour and how, if she had felt like hitting him, then she had also laughed with him, she went out on to her balcony.

In seconds she was lost in fascination of the panorama of the frozen Lake Baikal. The wind had swept snow into light drifts over the ice, she saw, and to her mind the picture appeared like a frozen sea with frozen white waves upon it.

She gazed and gazed, and then, looking at the trees near to the hotel, and then at the granite-looking mountain range way over beyond the lake, she was suddenly taken by a yearning to investigate.

The Siberian cold biting through her indoor clothing, however, made her quickly return to her 'desk'. But having tasted a glimpse of what was out there, she was all at once itching to get away from the hotel to explore.

Instead she stayed where she was, pounding the typewriter keys and resenting with all she had that since the report she was typing would not be needed until they were back in England, it could quite well have waited. But no, she fumed, 'tomorrow' was not good enough for Mr Cheyne I-want-it-done-yesterday Templeton. Whatever happened, be he working in the Sahara or in Eastern Siberia, he would not allow work to go undone.

Jolene typed the last full stop on her transcribed shorthand at five-thirty that afternoon. She was seated in an easy chair taking what she considered a well-earned breather when, at a quarter to six, there was a tap on the door of the suite.

She guessed who it was, and went to the door experiencing an unexpected sense of achievement that if Cheyne Templeton had come to see how the work was progressing, she could tell him she had finished it.

'In a better humour?' he queried as she opened the door to him, and immediately she was having to grasp for self-control. One of these days...she thought as without a word she left him to follow her to the sitting-room-cum-office. 'You've been busy, I see,' he commented as he glanced at the table and saw her neatly stacked typed-back pages.

Jolene disdained to feel warmed that he had noticed, and stared past him at the alluring picture outside her window. 'Some of us have worked all afternoon,' she told him aloofly, and discovered that either he did not like her tone, or her, or both, when he rapped aggressively,

'Accept my apologies. I'm afraid it escaped me completely that you regard this as your annual holiday!'

'That's most unfair!' Jolene dropped her aloof manner to fire up angrily. 'I've worked hard for you virtually since our plane landed in Moscow. I saw nothing of Moscow because your work had to come first, and I accept that. I saw nothing of Irkutsk either, for that matter...'

'But you would have done, regardless that Viktor Sekirkin has a wife. But I forget, you have a preference for married men, don't you, Miss Draper?' he snarled hostilely. 'You don't care...'

'I do *not* have a preference for married men!' Jolene almost yelled, so beside herself did this man make her. Desperately she fought for some control in what was degenerating into full-scale warfare. She gained control of her voice in so much as she was no longer yelling, but in doing so she sacrificed control of her tongue as she pitched the battle straight into his camp, saying stonily, 'Though of course we all know where your preference lies.'

'What the hell do you mean by that?' Cheyne snarled.

'What would I mean,' Jolene refused to back down, 'but that while everything's sweetness and light when you're talking to the PA you prefer, I, who am merely an acting PA, get the taciturn grumpy end? What would I mean,' she went on, any control she thought she had again getting away from her as she once more grew furious that he could so accuse her, 'but that you're hating it like blazes that Gillian Frampton isn't here with you now?'

'Gillian Frampton, for your information, is the best PA I've ever had,' he told her icily. 'For your further information, Miss Draper, she'd have whistled through the work which you've been hard at all afternoon, and anything else I had for her to do—and all,' he barked shortly, 'without complaint.'

'Well, she would, wouldn't she!' Jolene snapped, feeling stung, and even while part of her was urging that she was going too far, she did not seem to be able to stop herself going further. 'How sad that she couldn't come with you to Listvyanka, as you originally planned!'

'You seemed to have learned a lot in a short time,' he gritted. 'Did Gillian tell...'

'She didn't have to tell me! I'm not so stupid that I don't know that but for some—some hiccup, she'd have been with you here today. And that,' she charged furiously, 'is why you're ready to shoot me down any chance you can. Gillian Frampton couldn't come after all for some reason and, with your plans for a pleasant stay in Listvyanka gone up in smoke, you decided to take it out on...' her voice faded when she saw a glint of steel come to his eyes. Indeed, she was starting to wonder at her own temerity when Cheyne moved a furious pace nearer to her and stared with those steely eyes down into her sparking green ones.

'The reason why Gillian Frampton could not come on this very important trip,' he clipped, making no attempt to disguise that it was as Jolene suspected and that everything had been set originally for Gillian to be the fourth member of the party, 'is that she's pregnant.'

'Pregnant?' Jolene echoed, and as she felt the most dreadful feeling of inner disquiet at what she was hearing, she could no more refrain from asking the question that sprang into her mind than she could refrain from drawing her next breath. 'By you?' she charged, and as his hands suddenly clenched down by his sides, she was all at once doubting that she would be drawing another breath.

But although he took another angry pace nearer, Cheyne did not strangle her, as had looked likely, but, showing marked restraint, 'By her husband!' he snarled from between clenched teeth.

'Her husband?' echoed Jolene, completely stunned. 'I didn't know she was married!'

'There's quite a lot you don't know but which you prefer to guess at,' Cheyne erupted shortly. 'Gillian Frampton has been happily married for a number of years. And I—unlike you,' he fired, 'leave the opposite sex of the married kind alone!'

Quite what it was that made her do it, Jolene was not sure. But having been goaded off and on by him ever since she had met him, she decided that he had repeated that accusation once too often. Although at the time she was not thinking so clearly as to have a view of any kind, but, at his insistence that she was some married man-mad harpy, the slap which had been on its way to him for all that day suddenly got delivered.

In actual fact, she barely knew that she had hit him. For one moment he was standing over her with his jaw jutting at an aggressive angle, and the next moment her palm was stinging, and a split moment after that, he was reaching for her.

Unafraid, Jolene still refused to back down. She felt his iron hands grip her upper arms, and saw from the look in his eyes that he had it in mind to shake her until her teeth rattled.

Then suddenly, even as his grip on her tightened, the look in his eyes changed. And swiftly Jolene went from being unafraid to being...she knew not what. 'No!' she cried, but Cheyne was past listening to anything she had to say. All too clearly as his head began to come down, he had heard more than enough from her, and had just thought of a very effective way of shutting her up.

Jolene did not have a chance to utter another word. For no sooner had that 'No!' left her than Cheyne's warm and attractive mouth was over hers.

For about two seconds she was stunned into not doing anything. But when in the next two seconds his hands left her arms and his arms came fully about her, she came out fighting—that or, as his kiss began to do crazy things to her, be sunk without trace.

Though, in truth, she did not have much of a fight on her hands. And she guessed that Cheyne was already regretting his action, for as she started to push him furiously away, he dropped his arms from about her and took a step back.

Some of the ice had gone from his look, though, for all his voice was cold, when, referring to the slap she had just served him, 'That,' he ground out, 'is not the way to get promotion!'

'Well, I sure as Henry am not going to go to bed with you to get it!' she retaliated furiously.

'You should get the chance!' he told her arrogantly. The next sound she heard was the door of the suite being slammed, as he strode out.

CHAPTER FIVE

HAD she really hit the chairman of Templeton's? Had the chairman really kissed her? Jolene vividly remembered the feel of Cheyne Templeton's mouth over hers, and she knew there was nothing imaginary about the kiss. Nor, try to deny it though she might, was there anything imaginary about the memory of the crazy, abandoned way she had begun to feel inside, before she had found some will-power to push him away.

Needing something to do if she were to get him, and his kiss, out of her head, Jolene went and bathed and changed, then returned to the sitting-room to wonder why she had bothered. She was not going to go down to dinner, that was for sure—she had seen quite enough of that man for one day!

Wretched man! she was still fuming an hour later. She had only gone down to lunch out of a determination to show him that she was not the tiniest bit interested in him—all she'd got for her trouble was the feeling that as far as he was concerned, she did not exist. Let him dine by himself if he felt like that!

Damn him! she thought, and although she was not sure why she should be damning him she was quite sure she did not care a jot that, apart from her being his acting PA slave, he was otherwise unaware of her existence.

A minute or so later Jolene was having another attempt at analysing what it was about the brute of a man that he should so quickly bring out the worst in her. That slap she had served him had been on its way to him for some time, she accepted. Though perhaps it had been the sting of hearing him praise Gillian Frampton and her 'whistle through the work' efficiency that had goaded her beyond control.

All at once, as her thoughts went along the avenue of—good grief, I'm not jealous of Gillian Frampton's efficiency, for pity's sake—and wondering if she had been jealous of her in other respects, Jolene suddenly found that she was shying away from such ridiculous thoughts.

Instead she sent her thoughts back to how stunned she had been to learn that Gillian Frampton was not only pregnant but married! And, according to Cheyne, happily married, and had been so for a number of years.

Going into the bedroom across the hall, Jolene rummaged in her case for the paperback she had brought with her to read, but had not so much as had the time to pick up. Reflecting that she supposed it was not unknown for a married career woman to prefer being referred to as Miss—and she remembered that Cheyne had so referred to her on one occasion—Jolene again rummaged through her belongings. Finding the packet of biscuits she had brought with her 'just in case', she returned to the sitting-room and had just settled herself down when someone knocked at her door.

Because it might be her employer, and because, since he might want to check over the report she had typed, she might have to invite him in, Jolene went and dropped the biscuits back in her case before she opened the door.

Her heart did funny things inside her as she looked at the tall man on the other side of the door, then looked up into his cool dark grey eyes. The reason for her heart behaving so, though, she quite well knew, was that it was not every day that she took a swipe at the chairman, and it was not every day that he kissed her to shut her up—this being the first time she had seen him since then.

She swallowed, and, unsure whether to offer a sarcastic 'To what do I owe the pleasure?' or whether to simply turn and leave him to follow her to the 'office', Jolene discovered he was not giving her time to do either when, with his voice as cool as his look, he enquired, 'Sulking, or eating?'

Sulking! There he went again! What was it about this man...? Jolene fought hard for control, and then, 'I'm starving,' she replied sweetly. With a murmured, 'I'll just get my bag,' she ducked along the hall to collect it, though not before Cheyne had turned away—turned away, if she was not mistaken, smiling. Had she again amused the awful man?

He was not smiling when she joined him and secured her door. But the fact that she thought she had glimpsed a smile on his face somehow lightened her own mood.

He seemed in a pleasant enough humour, at any event, as they chose to walk down to the basement restaurant. Guessing, though, that since they had about another ten days to get through before they returned to England he was perhaps doing his part to get their working relationship on a more amicable footing, Jolene decided that, in that case, she could be as big as him.

Though they were tucking into their first course of a quaint mixture of Russian salad, hard-boiled egg with cream and some sort of nondescript stalks with onions and gravy before she had got herself on an even enough

plateau to enquire, politely, 'Will we be staying in
Listvyanka for very long, Mr Templeton?'

Hoping she had got it right and that they had signed
an unofficial truce, she was nevertheless ready for him
if he replied with some sort of sarcastic offering on the
lines of—why did she want to know, had she got some
married man lined up in her sights at Listvyanka?

But to her relief, not to say pleasure, her employer's
voice was not sarcastic but even and, dared she believe
it, a shade friendly, when he replied, 'Make it Cheyne,
Jolene,' and, while she was getting over that, 'You've
worked like a Trojan this past week...'

'I've...' Jolene interrupted him, staggered. 'You've
noticed I've worked my fingers down to stumps!'

'Didn't I say?' he queried, and because he was so
blatant, when he knew jolly well that not one crumb of
praise had he tossed her way, she could do no other than
burst out laughing.

She saw his eyes rest on the curving smile of her
mouth, but she felt happy suddenly. His eyes went from
her mouth to her merriment-filled eyes, and as he smiled
too, as if he liked what he saw, Jolene was again glad
she had been the one selected to take Gillian Frampton's
place.

'Perhaps I didn't,' he drawled, and returned to the
matter previously under discussion. 'But had I not been
impressed with the way you've coped, then I believe I
might not have forgotten to mention that.'

There was no 'believe' about it. Jolene *knew* it. Had
the work she had done for him not been up to scratch,
then without a doubt she would have heard about it.

Glowing under what she felt was a compliment, she
felt honour-bound at that moment to mention how un-

ceasingly he had put all his efforts into seeing that the meetings they had had progressed smoothly. 'But you've worked hard too,' she told him, realising only then that aside from being forever on the alert, he had worked doubly hard, because when all the talking was done, what did he do but return to the hotel and give her hours of dictation?

'That's true,' he agreed immodestly, and suddenly *he* was laughing, and Jolene was realising how she liked to see him laugh. It made his eyes crinkle at the corners, and made his strong firm mouth seem, sensitive somehow. 'Which is why,' he sobered to resume, 'I've decided to proclaim tomorrow a rest day.'

'A rest day?' she echoed, loving the sound of it. All at once, however, she suddenly realised that she was getting to know a little about this man. The word 'rest' she would have thought was not in his vocabulary. '*You* decided to have a rest day?' she queried, and again she liked it when he looked amused.

'To be more accurate, perhaps, it was Gillian's idea,' he conceded, and to her surprise, went on to explain, 'We were in the middle of mapping out the itinerary for this tour when I realised that, rather than have my engineers feel I was breathing down their necks, it might be better if I got out of the way while they got down to doing the work they specialise in.'

'Gillian Frampton suggested Listvyanka?' Jolene put in.

'She did,' Cheyne agreed, and as their first course dishes were cleared away and they were served their main course, he told her, 'Though I've an idea she spent the weekend leafing through some travel guides before she came to me and said she'd found what seemed a very nice spot to catch one's breath.'

Feeling more free than she ever had to discuss absolutely anything with him, Jolene questioned 'And you—agreed?'

'I may have mentioned that they don't come any smarter than Gillian at her job,' he murmured drily. 'Aside from the way she's worked long, hard, and for the most part without complaint for me this last five years, to agree to her suggestion when I knew she'd be—er—to quote "working her fingers down to the stumps" on this undertaking seemed no more than only fair.'

Feeling good inside to have him quote her remarks back with a smile, Jolene no longer felt a whit jealous of Gillian Frampton's professional ability. Besides, she was still glowing from hearing how Cheyne was impressed with the way she had coped.

So it was entirely without professional jealousy that after a moment or two she said, 'I expect Gillian was hating it like anything that, having arranged everything for this mission, she then couldn't come herself.'

'Not a bit of it,' Cheyne replied easily. 'Given that she's having a sickly time of it at present, she's wanted to become pregnant for so long that when it looked as though her dearest wish might come true, she didn't hesitate to take the action she did.'

'I'm sorry about her being poorly, but how lovely for her,' Jolene smiled, a gentle smile, and then, seeing the droll way Cheyne was looking, as though to say that women going ga-ga over babies or the expected arrival of one did not do very much for him, she mentally shook herself and shared with him, 'Because I did Russian at school, I was selected to stand by, but I was beginning to think I'd dreamt it all when an age went by and I never heard another word about it.'

'She regretted that,' Cheyne told her. 'But what with me being away, and Gillian not wanting to confide in anyone her hope that she was pregnant in case she was disappointed again, all she knew for sure at that stage was that by no chance was she going to take the risk of flying. Flying and early pregnancy don't mix, apparently,' he informed her.

'Don't they?' Jolene questioned, and discovered that he knew as little as her about the subject, seemingly, when he shrugged.

'So Gillian tells me. Anyhow, she knew that there was quite a lot of flying involved, so, since she's an efficient soul and since she also knew that I insisted, out of courtesy to our Russian friends, that each member of my party should have some degree of Russian, she arranged in my absence to have a Russian-speaking secretary put on standby. Because she was in a state of nerves about her was-she, wasn't-she condition, though, she didn't tell Personnel any of the whys and wherefores, but insisted they gave you only minimal information in case her hopes were again dashed and she herself would be on the Moscow flight.'

With her sympathy going out to the PA whose efficient and capable exterior must have covered a good deal of inner anguish after her setbacks in her desire to have a child, Jolene was silent for a moment or two.

Then, 'Like Alec and Keith, Gillian took a course in Russian too, didn't she?' she thought to ask.

Cheyne nodded in confirmation, and said, 'As you might expect, she proved herself a brilliant pupil too.'

'Naturally,' Jolene smiled, but there was not a scrap of animosity in her heart. Some people, she knew, were born gifted. By the sound of it, Gillian Frampton was one. Most definitely, Cheyne Templeton was another. Put the gifts he was born with together with his ability to work ceaselessly, and what had you got but a formula for success.

They finished their main course of veal, potatoes and beetroot, and Jolene caught Cheyne eyeing the cake that was to follow as if to wonder whether he'd rather remain still slightly hollow inside or whether to sacrifice himself.

'What's it taste like?' he asked as she cut into hers and took a trial bite.

'Lovely,' she told him, wide-eyed and innocent.

'Then you shall have mine too,' he offered gallantly, and suddenly they were both grinning. As cakes went, Jolene thought, she had tasted better.

After coffee, they left the dining-room and began to walk back up the stairs. Jolene was remembering how Cheyne had decreed that tomorrow be a rest day, and she had her thoughts on how she would take full advantage of that to do more than just look out from her balcony when she realised that he had never answered her question, 'Will we be staying in Listvyanka for very long?'

'What happens the day after tomorrow?' she suddenly asked him out of the blue, then felt bound to qualify, 'I seem to have only the barest outline of the itinerary you spoke of. I know we're going to Leningrad at some time, but . . .'

'I'm sorry,' he apologised handsomely. 'Gillian, as you can imagine, as well as keeping her eye on a few things for me in my absence, had a hundred and one other things on her mind before we left. You'll have to forgive her if she's overlooked a few other matters here and there, she...'

'I'm not carping or complaining,' Jolene assured him quickly. That Gillian had forgotten the small item of letting her have a copy of their itinerary was as nothing compared to the work the woman—sickly into the bargain—must have done in getting them flights and hotels and visas.

'I didn't think you were,' Cheyne assured her, and went on to fill in some of the blanks. 'The day after tomorrow we'll return to Irkutsk to see if Edwards and Shaw are having any problems I should know about. From there, you and I will make for Novosibirsk, where...'

That they were going to some place called Novosibirsk registered with Jolene, but what registered more particularly was what he had said before that. 'You and I?' she cut in to query. 'Aren't Keith and Alec coming with us?'

'At one time they were,' he replied. 'I've since then decided that their time will be more profitably spent if they extend their stay in Irkutsk. We're now re-scheduled to meet up with them in Moscow.'

'What about Leningrad?' she enquired. 'Do we all fly from Moscow there, and from there home?'

'You're in a hurry to get home for some reason?' he questioned sharply.

'Not at all!' Jolene answered crisply, wondering where his good humour had so abruptly disappeared to. 'I merely put the question,' she added stiffly, 'because you know where we're going, and I don't.'

'Of course,' he replied, and had such an assumed air of apology about him that Jolene nearly burst out laughing again, her equilibrium restored when he went on to enlighten her, 'Edwards and Shaw have no business in Leningrad, so you and I will go there first, then fly to Moscow, and from there the four of us will return to England.'

'But, before any of that, you have business in Novosibirsk,' she checked back, the stiffness gone from her voice as he escorted her to the door of her suite.

'Correct,' he confirmed.

'Will we be touring another factory there?' she asked, trying hard to look as though the idea filled her with enthusiasm.

But Cheyne was already shaking his head, and there was a definite gleam of good humour in his eyes, she thought, when he told her, 'You'll be relieved to know that we'll be in Novosibirsk attending a two-day conference,' and tacked on drolly, 'If you're very good, I'll let you take notes.'

Knowing full well that there would be blood on the moon—hers—if she did *not* take notes—the whole purpose of his taking her to Novosibirsk with him— Jolene turned, trying to hide her smile. She inserted her key in her door lock, and owned that she had never felt more light-hearted.

She was unsure, though, as she turned back to him, whether he intended to come into the 'office' for anything. But, since she had an apology outstanding to be made, she thought that right then was as good a time as any.

'I owe you an apology,' she told him prettily, as she looked up into his dark grey eyes. 'I was very much out of order to even think what I did about your—er—relationship with Gillian Frampton outside the office, let alone say it.' Her eyes were large and luminous as, sincerely, she told him, 'I'm sorry.'

Cheyne kept his eyes on hers, and the serious way he looked at her did the most peculiar things to her insides. Yet, although they now seemed to be sailing through calmer waters, he still had the most uncanny knack of making her usually serene self volatile, when he murmured, 'With charm like that, it's no wonder that you're always in trouble!'

'Are you being funny?' she bridled in a second, knowing at once that he was either referring to her trouble with Tony Welsh, or Viktor Sekirkin, or for that matter, any married man who came near her.

But, as instantly as he could make her temper soar, so it seemed that he could as instantly make her feel light-hearted again. 'Pax!' he grinned suddenly, and his eyes had gone to her mouth when, because she simply could not help it, she just had to break into a grin herself. Cheyne took a step back, and settled the issue of whether or not he intended to do some work that night when he bade her quietly, 'Goodnight, Jolene.'

'Goodnight—Cheyne,' she replied, and she entered her room with a dreamy smile on her face, and with the knowledge in her heart that he had charm too—when he cared to use it.

That night Jolene had the best night's sleep she had had since she had been in the Soviet Union. She awoke the next morning feeling refreshed and happy. And as she gazed out of her window she could barely wait to get bathed and dressed, because today she was not going to merely look and yearn to be out there, she was actually going to go and use her rest day in having a look outside.

Quickly she completed her ablutions and then, because common sense decreed that though she might be thermally clad, to eat a good breakfast might keep her insides warm in what had to be a good deal colder than twenty below out there, she went to eat.

She went down to the ground floor in the lift, and because it seemed that that was as far as that particular lift went, she stepped from the lift and was walking across the hotel lobby when, from nowhere, it seemed, Cheyne Templeton appeared.

'Good morning.' His greeting was friendly and the charm she had attributed to him last night was still there.

'Good morning,' she replied lightly, and her inner happiness moved on to a higher plane when his hand came to her elbow and clearly making for the restaurant too, he guided her to the basement staircase.

'I should eat plenty,' he instructed, as he handed her a plate of cheese slices. 'It's bitter out there.'

'You've been out?' Jolene enquired, as she accepted the cheese and passed him the plate of tasty dark brown bread.

'Only to test the temperature,' he replied. 'I thought of taking a walk after breakfast.' He paused to accept a slice of bread from the plate and then, looking across at her, 'Care to come?' he invited.

'Yes, please,' she replied without hesitation, and they both got busy with bread, butter and cheese, and with bits of 'shop' and bits of 'weather' thrown in, they went on to eat delicious frankfurter sausage, filling the last remaining corner with some bread and jam.

Once they had drunk their coffee, it was by mutual consent that they left the restaurant to return to the floor on which they had their rooms. Ten minutes later Jolene, trousered and sheepskin-clad, was meeting Cheyne again. She was too taken with how terrific her employer looked dressed for the outdoors to be aware of the very attractive picture she herself made with the white collar of her jacket complementing her skin, while the classic style of her sheepskin hat gave her a certain chic.

'Are you sure you've enough layers on?' Cheyne queried before they set off.

'Quite sure,' Jolene told him, itching to be off.

The hotel lay high in the hills, and fresh snow fallen during the night was all around as she and Cheyne left the hotel and followed a downward path. Trees abounded everywhere, and in the clean crisp air it was like nowhere she had ever been.

'No need to ask if you're enjoying this,' Cheyne smiled to her at one point as they progressed on their walk. Jolene realised then that her face must have been fairly expressive, but, with that feeling of happiness that had awakened with her still there, she could do nothing to hide the fact that she was enjoying every moment of this, her rest day.

Whether it was that she was so happy, or so interested in all that there was to see, or if something else was responsible, Jolene could not have said, but that morning simply flew by.

In the late morning they looked round a harbour filled with huge tankers and merchant ships which were packed in by solid ice. Nothing was moving, she saw, and minute upon swiftly flying minute went by as Cheyne helped her on to the ice, and they went to take a close look at the giant ships in their iced-in harbour.

A short way from the ships Jolene spotted a kiosk selling postcards and a few other oddments. 'Won't be a moment,' she told Cheyne, and because she wanted a memento of this visit she went and bought a picture postcard and also a plastic comb.

'Ready to make our way back?' asked Cheyne when she walked back to him with her purchases. And then, when although she was aware that by then it must be nearly lunchtime she would willingly have missed her lunch, he made her day by adding, 'Since today's a holiday, we could go for another walk this afternoon.'

'Seems like a sound scheme,' she murmured, and with her heart singing she had no space or wish to query— would she be enjoying this day so much, if she were there with someone other than Cheyne?

Lunch was a filling meal that began with raw fish, hard-boiled eggs and potato salad, followed by soup, then a mouthwatering veal, cheese and onion concoction which was served with an 'entertaining' version of chips, and beetroot.

By unspoken mutual consent, they took a short break after lunch, but just when Jolene was starting to get anxious that if they did not start out on their walk soon the light would be fading before they got very far, Cheyne came and knocked at the door of her suite. Having forgotten to take her camera with her that morning, she paused only to grab hold of it, then went to the door.

Again they took the road that led downwards. And again time sped by as, in between absorbing everything that there was to be seen, they discussed books, music and paintings, and talked in general on any subject that came up.

Then they came across a whole village of little wooden bungalows nestling at the foot of huge forest-covered hills, and suddenly Jolene was awestruck. Gazing in enchantment, she saw where each self-contained dwelling was individually fenced off and had its own garden, which at that time of the year was covered under a blanket of snow. Some gardens had tall trees growing in them, she observed, and while almost every house had a television aerial and there were telegraph poles and telephone wires to be seen, the whole area seemed not of this world, but magical and from another time.

So much so that even though Jolene knew that she was in Siberia, and knew that Lake Baikal must be but within stone-throwing distance, as too must be Listvyanka, she just had to ask, a hushed note in her voice, 'Where *is* this place?'

'I think it's called the village of St Nicholas,' Cheyne answered, and as he looked down into her enraptured face, 'If my attempt at Russian conversation didn't go badly awry just after lunch, I believe we'll find the church of St Nicholas at the top of this street. Would you like to try it?'

'Please,' Jolene said simply, and had plenty to occupy her both mentally and physically as she and Cheyne began to walk over what appeared to be a pavementless street.

Realising that while she was up in her suite after lunch he must have been occupied in making enquiries regarding the locality, Jolene was also realising just why he had phrased his suggestion in the terms he had. For as they walked on through what she had thought was the main street of the village, she soon began to have second thoughts about that. Because as the street began to widen out, it became her firm view that they must be walking over what must be a Russian version of the village pond.

'It's sheer ice underneath this snow!' she exclaimed when, but for Cheyne taking a quick hold of her arm when her feet started to go from under her, she felt sure she would have executed a very inelegant *pas de basque* with a splits finish.

'I know,' he murmured, and there was laughter in his eyes as, keeping a firm hold on her arm, he steered her over the ice for quite some distance, until they reached the picket fencing that surrounded the church and its grounds.

'I must take a picture!' Jolene exclaimed, taking her camera from around her neck, and, careless that Cheyne might think her 'touristy', she focused on the small natural wood church with its snowy top and green spire. When she pressed the shutter button, though, nothing happened, and when another two times she pressed it and still nothing happened, 'It worked perfectly all right the last time I used it,' she told Cheyne.

'That's because you weren't in Siberia and it wasn't the month of March,' he replied, and when she looked at him as though to ask what that had got to do with the price of haddock, 'Quite obviously your camera's frozen up,' he told her.

'Obviously,' Jolene replied, when the only thing that clicked was that she should have thought of that possibility for herself. But, seeing that there was an amused look in his eyes, she added, 'How did you get to be so clever?'

'Some have brilliance thrust upon them,' he murmured, trying to look modest, and failing—blatantly. Jolene grinned.

Her inner happiness was overflowing when he helped her negotiate a most treacherous-looking icy spot by the church gate. No sooner were they through the gate, however, than they saw a well wrapped up woman coming from an adjacent house to enquire if they wished to see inside of the church.

'May we?' Jolene asked Cheyne.

'I think we've just time, if we're to get back to the hotel while the light holds,' he replied, and as he addressed the woman, who Jolene thought must be the caretaker, the little church of St Nicholas was being opened up for them.

Before they went inside, though, Cheyne took hold of a brush made from twigs, about two feet long, which stood in the entrance. First he brushed the snow from Jolene's boots, then he attended to his own, then they went inside the tiny church, that had no pews except for a couple of benches along the back wall, which Jolene guessed must be for the aged and the infirm.

Jolene felt good inside, calm, and still very happy as she thanked the woman for opening up and Cheyne offered a donation, then they left the church.

Outside she looked down the way they had come and the way they must return, and again the magic of the place crept over her.

Cheyne's hand was once more beneath her elbow as they negotiated the treacherous ice by the gate, and walked on to negotiate the rest of the way which, for all it seemed less treacherous, was nevertheless still ice.

Suddenly, though, when they were about half-way down the street-cum-frozen pond, Jolene felt as though she had to say something—anything. Quite what was the matter with her she had no clue, but when a companionable sort of silence had fallen between them, all at once she found herself breaking out into panicky speech.

'I wonder...' Her voice faded, but, getting herself more together, having broken the silence, she had to find something to say that might appear sensible. 'Did you explore this way yesterday afternoon?' she pulled out of thin air, some part of her subconscious recognising that Cheyne was too active a man to sit doing nothing in his hotel room if he was not working.

'Yesterday afternoon, like you, I worked,' he told her as they skirted another patch of waiting-for-victims ice.

'You worked!' she exclaimed in some surprise. To date it had been her lot to get the backlash of any work which Cheyne did outside of a meeting, but she had seen nothing of yesterday's efforts.

'I thought I'd better formulate a few ideas on to paper if I'm not to drone my audience to sleep.' Ever a man to astonish, he did it again.

'What audience?' Jolene questioned, stopping dead in her tracks.

With his steadying hand still on her arm, Cheyne came to a halt too. 'Didn't I say?' he queried, and when he could see from her expression that he had not, 'I'm one of the speakers at the conference in Novosibirsk,' he said casually.

He might well have moved on then, but Jolene was standing as though rooted. This man was so full of surprises. There was so much that she did not know about him. And suddenly, as she looked at him, she knew that she wanted to know more about him—much, much more, because, suddenly, she knew exactly why she had felt so happy all day. Suddenly, too, she knew that that knowledge trying to break through was the reason for her panic a short while ago.

Feeling stunned, and winded, she stared at him from saucer-round serious green eyes. And then, as Cheyne looked seriously back at her, he smiled a gentle smile as though to say he was enjoying her company. Then all at once they had moved a step nearer to each other, and who reached for whom she had no idea, but she was suddenly in his arms, and his wonderful mouth was over hers in a warm and gentle kiss.

Then, when her heart was full to bursting, he was breaking that kiss, taking a step back from her. And while Jolene was floundering in an emotion of which she had no prior experience, she unconsciously made a shaky involuntary movement. Then he was bringing her back to earth by calmly reminding her that they were in a village in Siberia, and that they were standing on snow-covered ice.

'Steady, Jolene,' he murmured, as with his hand again on her elbow, he turned her in the direction they should go, 'we can't have you falling.'

Automatically, Jolene moved one foot after the other, but his warning had come too late. She had already fallen—in love with him!

CHAPTER SIX

JOLENE sat in the bedroom of her hotel suite early that evening, and no longer wondered why it was that Cheyne Templeton could cause her to react so against the nature of the person she had thought herself to be. She was in love with him—and, she had realised, it must have been coming on ever since they had met. He had stirred emotion in her from the very first, at any rate.

Wishing she had a more extensive wardrobe with her, she selected the red two-piece as the best she had brought to do duty at dinner that evening. Because by then the time was going on, she had a hurried bath and, having quickly dried and dressed, she bemoaned the fact that her thick blonde hair, which had looked perfectly all right before she had known herself in love, looked anything but all right now.

Realising that her hands were shaking and that she had got herself into something of a dither, Jolene took a few minutes out to calm herself.

With the exception of her discovering why it was that Cheyne could make her heart behave in such a peculiar fashion, nothing had outwardly changed, she lectured herself. Her day had been a happy one and, given that she had a natural reserve about making displays of affection, it was highly unlikely that she would suddenly throw her arms around Cheyne and embrace him the instant she saw him again. Well, not unless he made some display of wanting to embrace her first, anyhow.

For a second or two she drifted off into a dream where Cheyne came to call to take her down to dinner, but, because he felt the same way that she did, he was unable to prevent himself from taking her in his arms.

That dream faded when reality presented itself. Apart from their sense of humour being on the same wavelength occasionally, she had seen not one single solitary sign that Cheyne might be remotely in love with her. Oh, he had kissed her a couple of times, but one of those kisses had been to shut her up, the other...

Foolishly Jolene drifted off again to remember once more how happy she had been that day and how Cheyne had seemed to like her company.

When the minutes had ticked by and her watch showed the same time that Cheyne had called for her the previous evening, she was ready and waiting. She had realised the folly of hoping that he might be a little in love with her, but by then she had sifted through his every 'non-work' word said to her in a search to discover if perhaps he liked her a little. By then she had seen his warning 'Steady, we can't have you falling' as stemming not from any thought that he would be mightily inconvenienced if she was injured and unable to act as his PA, but from the fact that—perhaps—he was getting to like her a little and did not want her to hurt herself.

The answer to whether he had any feelings for her, however small, began to filter in when ten minutes went by and Cheyne did not come and knock on her door.

Jolene let a few more minutes go by, then thought very briefly about going to knock on his door before instantly discarding the idea, then she thought for another two minutes before quickly leaving the suite.

She made her way down to the restaurant, having come
to the speedy conclusion that it would be better for her
to put in an appearance at dinner. That way she could
better gauge his attitude, whereas, if she stayed in the
suite, she would only go through the torture of wondering did he or did he not think anything, however
small, of her.

The answer to that hit her cruelly straight between the
eyes the moment she entered the dining-room. For any
faint notion she might have nursed that he might be
working and had lost count of the time evaporated into
thin air when she saw that he was already at the table.

'Good evening,' she said pleasantly, when as she
reached the table he stood up.

His grunt in greeting was all she needed to know that
the holiday, the rest day was over, and that he was back
to being the same surly brute she was more familiar with.

What she ate at that meal Jolene had no recollection.
But she thanked God for her pride that, although part
of her wanted to beg for one kind word from Cheyne,
there was another part, a stronger part, that said, 'Like
hell!'

Somehow, when all she wanted was to return to her
room to lick her wounds, she made herself stay right
where she was. She drank her coffee, the final part of
the meal, as if she had not a care in the world, and had
no mind at all to dash to the upstairs suite and close the
door.

She was in the middle of wondering what the dickens
had happened to change him from the warm and
charming man she had seen that day to the uncommunicative swine he was now, when suddenly, not waiting for
her, he stood up and seemed about to go.

'We're leaving in the morning—be on time,' he clipped by way of a goodnight.

'I'll be delighted,' she said sweetly, and when he gave her a sour look at her impudence, she smiled.

She was not smiling when he had gone, however. For she had seen the way his eyes had flicked to her mouth, and suddenly she knew just why he had reverted to being such a taciturn swine.

Jolene returned to her rooms weighed down by the embarrassment her realisation had brought. Quite plainly, she must have responded too eagerly to his kiss that afternoon. Equally plainly, Cheyne was now regretting the impulse that had prompted him to take her in his arms, and, without a doubt, he was now hell-bent on getting their relationship back on a businesslike foundation.

By morning Jolene, after a dreadful night, had surfaced to be certain that Cheyne Templeton need not put himself out. A businesslike basis would suit her just fine. She had not asked him to take her in his arms—he could go boil his head!

Cheyne was already down to breakfast when she entered the hotel's restaurant, and just the sight of him, broad-shouldered and manly, briefly scattered her brave thoughts. She recovered, however, when, certain courtesies being inbred in him, apparently, he got to his feet and remained standing until she had taken her place at the table.

When his inbred courtesy did not extend to him finding a civilised greeting for her, Jolene decided that even a relationship of purely the business kind deserved an exchange of good mornings.

So, 'Good morning', she bade him pleasantly and as if she had not so much as missed a wink of sleep on his account last night. And, not giving him time to answer, 'Could I ask you to pass the pork, please?' asked she, who did not feel like eating a crumb, and certainly not cold pork, no matter how thinly sliced.

Her employer was not in a sunny humour that morning. Jolene could not have cared less. It was definitely raining on her parade. Far from wanting to return to Irkutsk, she wanted to return to England. Yet there was still over a week to be got through before they got on that plane in Moscow.

It did not help matters that the taxi which was coming from Irkutsk to pick them up was late. Having made a point of being on time herself as ordered, Jolene left her luggage in the foyer and went window-shopping. From what she could make out there appeared to be a Beriozka store in every hotel, which sold things as varied as beautiful large fringed shawls, and different varieties of vodka.

It was nearer eleven than ten when the taxi finally arrived, and the return trip took them an hour and a quarter. They returned to the same hotel they had vacated two days earlier, but were booked into different rooms from the ones they had previously occupied, though again they were both on the same floor.

By the time the porter was taking them with their luggage up to their floor, however, Jolene, having exercised all her resources in trying to remain pleasant to her monosyllabic employer, felt used up. When the lift stopped, she followed the porter to her allocated room. Thanking the porter when he had carried her case into her room, but without a word to her employer, she went to close the door on both of them.

'We'll lunch at one,' Cheyne told her curtly before she could achieve her intention.

'I can't wait,' she found some stray particle of unused-up strength to tell him guilelessly.

She saw his eyes narrow and as he stared at her harshly, she felt sure he was about to tell her to cut the impudence. She closed the door.

To her utter relief, Alec Edwards and Keith Shaw were there when at one o'clock precisely she entered the dining-room. All three men at the table for four got to their feet when she arrived, and she felt warmed to her heart when first Alec took her right hand in his and then pecked her right cheek as though a bond of friendship had grown between them, and then Keith did the same. Her glance then lit on the third man in the group, but from his grim look she could tell that he had not sweetened up in any way.

'How are things going?' she asked the two engineers generally when they were all seated and sampling the beetroot, cream and cheese starter.

'So far so good,' Alec told her, 'though we've a good way to go yet, I imagine,' and turning to Cheyne, he said, 'Keith and I have kept the afternoon free hoping that we could have a meeting. If you can spare the time, Mr Templeton, I should value your opinion.'

With her ear to the conversation, but taking no active part, Jolene disposed of the soup course, and munched her way through the course that followed. For light relief, instead of the more usual cake to follow, there was ice cream.

'This is good,' she remarked to Keith, about her whole contribution to the lunchtime table conversation. But, having found her voice, and finding too when she looked across at Cheyne that he had his glance on her, 'Will you need me this afternoon, Mr Templeton?' she asked him politely, having formed the view from the conversation she had heard that they would manage very well without her.

For perhaps two seconds he looked hard at her while, unblinking and trying to pretend that there had never been a time when she had used his first name, Jolene stared back at him. Then, when she was expecting something sharp from him along the same lines as his jibe about her thinking this trip was her annual holiday, he said, quite pleasantly, 'Take the afternoon off, Jolene, I've no need of you.'

That just about summed it up, she thought when later she took her purse down to the Beriozka with the intention of making a few purchases. Cheyne had no need of her. Any PA could have done what she had done so far, she saw that clearly enough.

Well, he could stay a grouch as far as she was concerned! her pride came to give her a nudge, as she purchased a bottle of vodka to take home to her father. By then she had realised that the only reason his voice had been in any way pleasant to her anyhow was that Keith and Alec had been present. Her pride slipped a little so that she was liking Cheyne again in that, whatever he thought about the eagerness of her response to his kiss, he would not make her feel small in front of the others.

Putting Cheyne firmly out of her mind, she set about buying a large shawl for her mother. Then, because she could not resist them, she bought three nests of wooden dolls, one for her mother, one for her neighbour, and one for herself—hadn't Alec told her that brightly painted dolls with their sarafan dress and headscarves were called Matryoshka, which was the forename of the wife of the original carver. With her presents neatly wrapped, Jolene was in the middle of taking her change from the sterling notes with which she had made her purchases when a voice from behind called 'Jolene!'

Swinging round, she saw that Viktor Sekirkin had come into the hotel and had spotted her at the far end of the foyer where the Beriozka was situated. '*Dobriy dyehn*, Viktor,' she smiled.

'Good afternoon, Jolene,' he returned, and he was more grinning than smiling when he said, 'We will speak in English, I need the practice,' and straight away followed up, 'I knew it was you as soon as I came through the hotel door.'

'You have remarkable eyesight,' she told him.

'You have remarkable blonde hair,' he replied, and while his eyes made a meal of her shiny blonde hair, 'You will come and have a cup of coffee with me?' he invited.

'I don't think so, Viktor,' she told him affably, but found him very persuasive when he insisted.

'But yes, you must. There is a bar here on this floor in the hotel.'

About to attempt to refuse again, Jolene wondered if she was perhaps being a little ridiculous. He was only inviting her to drink a cup of coffee with him, for heaven's sake! Knowing that he'd probably laugh his little Russian socks off if she trotted out something unsophisticated like, 'I'm sorry, I can't have a cup of coffee

with you because you're a married man', Jolene knew
she would feel equally ridiculous saying it.

Which was why in the next minute she was going with
Viktor to check in his hat and coat at the ground-floor
cloakroom and then going with him to what he termed
a bar. From what she could make out, though, there was
nothing alcoholic served there.

'You are not working this afternoon?' Viktor queried
as soon as they were sitting with their coffee before them.
'Please say that you have not to rush off to work!' he
added quickly.

'I have the afternoon off,' Jolene told him. 'How
about you, aren't you working?'

'Oh, I don't work all the time,' he told her with a
broad smile, and then suddenly he started to look very
earnest as he went on, 'But this is wonderful, Jolene! If
you are not working, and I am not working, it is a most
perfect opportunity for me to take you on the sightseeing of Irkutsk which I wished to do before.'

Oh, crumbs! Jolene thought, and knew then, ridiculous or not, that she was going to have to tell him thanks,
but no, thanks. 'Er——' she began as she sought round
for tact. 'Actually, Viktor,' she was forced to go on when
she could see from his waiting expression that she had
the floor, 'the thing is . . .' she began, and again faltered.
'I'm . . .' There was nothing else for it, she realised when
she again dried. 'You're married,' she said bluntly.

'Divorced,' he smiled.

'I'll get my coat and hat,' she told him.

She enjoyed Viktor's company that afternoon. He was
easy to get along with and she welcomed having something else to think of other than Cheyne, when Viktor
took her first to an art gallery.

'Perhaps you will like some of the paintings,' he suggested as, first going to the cloaks area, they divested themselves of their topcoats and hats, where a lady attendant hung them up.

'I'm sure I shall,' Jolene smiled, and sauntered with him from room to room, where in each room sat a lady attendant of mature years.

As was the case with any other art gallery she had been to, Jolene liked some of the paintings, found others tolerable, and hated a few. But as they left the gallery Cheyne was back in her thoughts again.

She realised then that to tell herself to forget him was one thing, but that to actually go more than fifteen minutes without him springing, unsought, into her mind was totally another. Perhaps it would be easier when she was back in England and stood little or no chance of ever being in his company, she mused, when, because she could do nothing about it, Cheyne kept her mental company as Viktor that afternoon took her to the places he thought might be of interest to her.

At Victory Square she stood with him and watched as senior schoolchildren marched to keep guard over the Eternal Flame. 'They'll freeze if they stay there too long,' Jolene fretted as she and Viktor left the scene.

'They will be there for only ten minutes, and then other children selected for the honour will come to take their places,' he assured her.

Thinking that the Siberian people must be a hardy race, Jolene had more proof of that when, as she and Viktor were looking at another monument to fallen heroes, a bride, with her new husband, came to lay her bouquet. Moving away from the pretty young woman,

Jolene thought she must be nearly frozen in her fine white bridal gown.

The bride, though not the wedding, went from her thoughts however when, as she and Viktor left the monument, she noticed the car which the bridal couple had arrived in. For the car was white, and whether that was traditional or not Jolene did not know, but what was traditional, she felt sure, and in her view was rather nice, was that the roof of the car was decorated with two upright intertwined wedding rings. Through the larger wedding ring was threaded a white ribbon which went from the back to the front of the car, and through the smaller wedding ring, threaded in matching fashion, ran a red ribbon.

Dearly wanting to know the significance, if any, of the ribbons, Jolene almost put the question to Viktor, but he was paying no heed whatsoever to the wedding car, and she was sensitive suddenly that what with him not being much more than thirty, and already divorced, perhaps he would rather not talk of such matters as weddings.

Irkutsk, she learned that afternoon, was founded on the banks of the river Angara, and she had a chance to see the Angara when she and Viktor left the Yuri Gagarin Boulevard, and stepped to the frozen water's edge.

'What's happening over there?' she enquired of her friendly guide, pointing to where little domes of clear plastic were dotted about on the ice.

'Men are fishing,' Viktor answered.

'Fishing?' she exclaimed. 'Through the ice?'

'But of course,' he smiled. 'They cocoon themselves in their plastic cases, and drill holes through the ice.'

'Of course,' she murmured, and as her eyes moved to the left, she was sure that either her eyes were deceiving her or that here, on the other side of the Urals, there on the ice was a huge model of the Sydney Opera House! 'It isn't!' she turned her astonished gaze to Viktor to exclaim, but when he offered to escort her over the ice to take a closer look, she declined the offer. She had walked over the ice with another man yesterday—the memory was suddenly painful. 'Perhaps I'd better be getting back to the hotel,' she suggested.

'It is not far,' he immediately acquiesced, but spent the time until they reached the hotel in trying to get her to go out with him again.

'I think there's a good chance that I'll be required to work this evening,' she turned down his invitation for that night, as having her hotel pass ready, Viktor escorted her past the man at the door and into the foyer.

'You will be free tomorrow?' he refused to take no for an answer.

'Most definitely I shall be working tomorrow,' Jolene smiled apologetically.

'In the evening too?' he exclaimed.

'Maybe not,' she had to concede. 'May I have your phone number, Viktor? I can give you a call if...'

'That is an excellent suggestion!' he immediately took up, and without more ado he went to the reception desk, asked for some paper, and quickly wrote down his telephone number.

Jolene took the piece of paper he had given her, and sincerely thanked him for his kindness that afternoon. In return Viktor shook her warmly by the hand and, with his eyes enjoying her face, told her that he would live for her phone call.

There was a smile on her lips as she walked away from him. Somehow she had never expected a Russian to be so extravagant in his turn of phrase. The smile was still on her lips as she rounded the corner to where the lifts were. At the sight of the tall, dark-haired, grim-looking Englishman who stood there, though, her smile quickly departed. And that was before he grated:

'It's to be hoped you haven't been giving any of our secrets away!'

Jolene no longer wondered what it was about this man that, when her heart had been aching over him on and off throughout the afternoon, her first sight of him should coincide with an urge to hit him. 'What do *I* know, for heaven's sake!' she erupted hotly.

'For a single woman of your young years, far more than you should!' he snarled, to make her hand itch again.

'For your information,' she hissed, 'I'm still a virgin!'

'Huh!' he scorned, and had the lift not come at that moment, and, had he not at that same moment moved, Jolene felt certain she would have hit him.

She rode up in the lift with him in fuming silence, and was damned if she'd ask him if he had any work for her. All too clearly he had seen her in the foyer with Viktor Sekirkin, and had taken a dim view of it.

Collecting her room key from the floor attendant, she went to her room with her heart full of mutiny. My godfathers! Was there ever such an impossible man!

She was still angry as she got washed and changed ready to go down to dinner, and although she knew that he had not believed her, she had to wonder why in creation she had let him goad her into telling him of her virgin state.

She went down to dinner that night having got herself well under control. She was coming to terms with the fact that quite obviously Cheyne Templeton had no time for her. Though it still rankled that plainly he did not trust her to keep the firm's confidences, she decided, in the interests of a harmonious dinner table, that she would not mention to either Alec or Keith that Viktor had shown her a little of the city that afternoon.

She had reckoned, however, without Alec killing the odd moment or two with doing a spot of window-watching, and having disposed of her first course, she was just cutting into a slice of beef when Alec chose to remember, and query, 'Didn't I see you crossing the road with Viktor Sekirkin this afternoon?'

What could she do? She made sure her glance did not flick in Cheyne's direction, and she smiled. 'Yes, you did,' she replied brightly. 'We did a mini tour of the city.'

She had hoped to end the conversation there, and had returned her attention to her beef, when Keith decided to add his two pennyworth. 'Trying to do your bit for Anglo-Russian relations, Jolene?' he enquired.

'He's a nice enough man,' she returned pleasantly, by then receiving grim vibes from the dark-haired man opposite her, and knowing that this conversation was not finding favour with him.

'He's an excellent engineer,' Keith responded, and as Jolene lifted her head, 'Going out with him again, Jo-Jo?' he teased.

As she was about to tell him in a friendly way that it was none of his business, the fact that he had so surprisingly hit on the version of her name which her parents sometimes used unexpectedly got to her. Her parents loved her, and right then Jolene felt in need of having someone love her.

'I have a—tentative—date with him tomorrow,' she told Keith, and was soon laughing when he went through the lists of dates he had had prior to his marriage, not one of them ever being a 'tentative' one.

The conversation had gone from her 'tentative' date to cover a few other subjects, and was on how the weather must either be getting warmer or they were acclimatising, when, their second course cleared away, Alec held the plate of cakes out to her.

'Any plans for tonight, Jolene?' he asked as she helped herself to a spongy cake with a lovely-looking gooey topping.

Instinctively her glance went to Cheyne, but when she saw the chips of ice in his eyes as, unsmilingly, he held her look, the idea of asking him if she would be working that night went straight out of her head.

Luckily, though, at that moment Keith chose to explain why Alec had put his question. 'Alec and I are thinking of taking a stroll around the place in half an hour or so. Would you like to come with us?' he asked.

Dragging her eyes away from Cheyne's icy expression, Jolene at that point felt she had just about had enough of him. 'Where will you be?' she asked, inwardly starting to fume that, devil take it, she might be in love with the wretched man, but she was nobody's doormat, to sit there afraid to be herself in case she offended him.

Jolene was still silently fuming as Keith told her that they would wait for her down in the lobby. Oh, she knew quite well what Cheyne was thinking, she thought furiously—he was thinking that, not content with one married man—and she'd be damned if she would tell him that Viktor was divorced—she was setting her cap at his two married engineers—both at the same time!

The four of them left the dining-room together and made for the lifts. Alec and Keith were housed several floors below the floor she and Cheyne were on, and got out at their floor with a mutual, 'We'll see you later.'

The grim silence in the lift when she had nothing to say to her employer, and he had nothing he wanted to say to her, did not cool Jolene's temper at all.

Since he had nothing to say to her, however, she was prepared to see him in hell before she would say one more word to him. Suddenly, though, as the lift stopped at their floor it became evident that he did have something to say to her.

Though, in her opinion, his words were more barked than said, when as they stepped out of the lift, he as good as ordered, 'It might be an idea if you cancelled your arrangement to join Edwards and Shaw and had an early night.'

It was one thing that she should know that she had lost a lot of sleep last night, but quite another that Cheyne Templeton should choose this moment to tell her she looked a wreck. 'Why?' she questioned belligerently.

'For the same reason you'll be cancelling your 'tentative' date with Sekirkin,' he commanded toughly. And when Jolene was about to bridle, his voice went suddenly silky, as he ended, 'You and I, Miss Draper, are catching the Trans-Siberian Express in the morning.' Her jaw had just about hit the carpet when he told her, 'We'll breakfast at eight.'

Jolene was still staring at him open-mouthed when, without another word, he walked away from her.

CHAPTER SEVEN

BY THE following morning Jolene had recovered from her immense surprise that she and Cheyne were to journey on the Trans-Siberian Railway. A small smile played around her mouth as she got out of bed and went to run her bath, for she could not deny that she felt a flicker of excitement at the idea.

She had still been shaken the previous evening, though, when first she had got through to Alec's room to tell him not to wait as she would not be joining him and Keith for their stroll around Irkutsk. After she had telephoned Alec she rang Viktor, as commanded, to tell him that she could not see him tomorrow, because she was leaving by train.

'You are saying that this is "goodbye" and I might never see you again?' he queried, sounding desolate and doing her pride a world of good to think that if one particular man of her acquaintance had no time for her, then that did not go for the whole male population.

'I'm afraid so,' she replied, knowing for sure that while Viktor might soothe her pride, his air of gloom was exaggerated. She rang off having promised that she would keep his phone number and that if she were ever in Irkutsk again, she would ring him immediately.

Having become aware that although it was bitterly cold outside, the central heating inside was excellent, Jolene calculated that the Russians would have seen to it that the interior of the train was no exception. For this reason she did away with her thermals and opted to wear layers rather than thick clothing, and after her bath she dressed in a comfortable pair of trousers and a crisp white blouse, topped with a thin sweater. She had a thin cardigan ready to put on for when she returned to her room after breakfast.

She saw a similarly lightweight-clad Cheyne Templeton leaving his room just as she came out of her room. Glad that she appeared to have got something right, she fiddled about securing her door, thinking that from what she knew of him, he was just as likely to walk past her as to wait for her.

But no, he seemed in a better humour this morning, for he bade her, 'Good morning,' and actually paused in his stride to wait for her to fall into step with him so they could walk to the lift together.

'Good morning,' she replied and added sweetly, 'Cheyne,' for no reason other than that she sometimes had the devil in her.

They went down in the lift with Jolene giving herself a little talking to on the subject of that little imp of mischief in her that would have to be severely suppressed. Not that Cheyne seemed to have taken any exception to her calling him by his first name—though since it was he who had invited her to use it, she did not see how he could, anyhow.

Breakfast was a more brisk affair that morning. As soon as the bread and cheese and boiled eggs were partaken of, Cheyne instructed her that the train was said to arrive punctually and depart punctually.

She returned to her room briefly to collect her belongings and discovered that Alec and Keith were on hand to help her with her luggage, and then it was all bustle, with Cheyne checking them out of the hotel, and Alec and Keith coming to the taxi to see them off.

'See you in a week's time,' Alec told her, as he kissed her cheek in parting, and Keith followed suit.

'Dah sveedahneeyah,' she told them, and at her Russian 'goodbye' the taxi moved off.

The flicker of excitement which had been with her since first thing that morning increased by leaps and bounds when at the railway station she walked with Cheyne down some concrete steps and was then well and truly among a throng of people all crushing together to get to the same train.

Her excitement soared when, after some minutes of walking through a kind of subway, the queue of people turned right, she among them, and there, to the left, was the train.

Jolene had no idea at all if their seats on the train were reserved, but since Cheyne seemed to know what he was doing, she went with him and stopped when he stopped. He was in the act of hefting their cases up into one of the coaches, though, when, as she went to give him a hand, she heard her name called in much the same fashion as yesterday afternoon.

She turned swiftly—and could barely believe her eyes, for there, with a single red rose in his hand, stood Viktor Sekirkin.

'Viktor!' she exclaimed, and because she felt that, although he was a flirt, he was otherwise perfectly harmless, she beamed a welcoming smile.

'I could not let you go without seeing you once more,' he said, to warm her bruised heart.

'Oh, Viktor,' she said softly, and was suddenly enfolded in a bear-hug.

Hurriedly she stepped back, and it was then that he handed her the red rose. 'For you,' he said and, making her smile as he piled on the flattery, 'No rose can compare with your beauty.'

It was on the tip of her tongue to make some laughing comment to the effect that he should have been a poet, when suddenly a harsh voice was grating, 'This train won't wait!'

Quickly Jolene clambered aboard, and had time only to wish him, '*Dah sveedahneeyah*, Viktor,' and then the conductress in charge of that particular coach was securing the door and the train was off.

With Viktor's rose in her hand Jolene walked up the coach until she found the compartment in which Cheyne stood stowing their luggage away. The compartment for their larger cases was way up high, but he was tall and athletic, and where a shorter or less fit person might have needed help, he had no such need.

When she was about to smile and thank him for stowing away her luggage, though, Jolene was suddenly struck by his hostile expression when his glance went from her face to the red rose in her hand.

Suddenly then that devil that had got out of her control earlier that morning was on the loose again. 'Who says romance is dead?' she trotted out sweetly.

'I wonder how many roses he gives his wife!' Cheyne shot back at her before she could blink, making Jolene aware, if she wasn't already, that his better humour had not stayed around for long.

'He's divorced!' she snapped, and, her sweet tone soon gone, she stared antagonistically at him for two seconds—then the rest of the compartment began to impinge.

Switching her gaze from him to look about her, she saw with something of a surprise that, although one could quite well sit in the compartment, it was made up of four bunks, an upper and a lower bunk on either side of where she was standing. With startled eyes she saw that in actual fact the compartment she was standing in was a sleeping compartment!

In the next few seconds it had logically registered with Jolene that the only reason for anyone to have a sleeping compartment was that they would be sleeping on the train. So why, awoke her surprised brain, had Cheyne Templeton put his luggage in here as well as hers? She thought, before they went any further, that it was about time she found out.

'What exactly,' she turned back to him to ask in a short tone, 'is your case doing in here?'

She had to give him full marks for being quick on the uptake, but no marks at all for charm when, giving her a look which she translated as meaning he thought she was being tiresome to say the least, 'At the risk of repeating myself,' he snarled, 'you're not my type!'

'Neither,' flared Jolene, hurt and not needing to have that rubbed in, 'am I sharing my bedroom with you!'

'Hell fire!' he roared, and went striding out of the compartment.

Hell fire to you too! Jolene mutinied as she went to the door to see where he was heading. She saw that he had buttonholed the conductress and guessed he was making arrangements to book a berth elsewhere.

Let him stew, she fumed as she went back into the compartment. She'd be hanged if she would go and help him out with his Russian. Going over to the half-curtained window, she looked out, but her thoughts were not on the snowy scene outside but on how, although she hoped Cheyne was getting into all sorts of a tangle with the Russian language, knowing him, he probably wasn't.

Swine of a man! she raged inwardly, still smarting from his remark about how she wasn't his type. She hoped his chickens died.

Suddenly she became aware that she still had Viktor's rose in her hand, and she moved away from the window. There was a small cloth-covered table in front of the window, she saw, and as well as holding a small dish of pre-wrapped biscuits, a lidded sugar bowl, and a bottle of mineral water, it was also decorated with a piece of greenery in a porcelain vase. The vase seemed the natural place for her rose. She decided against putting any water in the vase at this stage, but thought she would first check out just how rocky the train ride was going to be.

She was sitting on one of the lower bunks, that did daytime service as a carriage seat, and her indignation had quietened down to a steady simmer when Cheyne returned to block the doorway. Her anger with him was to go soaring again, however, when, looking up and expecting that at any moment his hands would be busy in taking his possessions out of there, she saw that they were already busy—holding two metal-framed glasses of tea!

Feeling ready to explode, and certain that even a novice could not get their Russian so confused that 'I'd like another compartment' came out sounding like 'I'd like a cup of tea', Jolene took a deep breath to begin seethingly, 'Didn't you...'

'Yes, I did!' he cut her off sharply as he placed the tea on the table. Bluntly then he went on, 'Remember "when in Rome"—well, you'll be pleased to hear that apparently it's quite usual on this railway for the sexes to mix in together with no one—save the odd foreigner—thinking anything more about it.'

'You mean I'm expected . . .'

'I mean that there's no chance of my finding alternative sleeping quarters,' Cheyne again cut her off, and before she could make anything out of that—and she was ready to—'The position is this,' he went on forcefully. 'This train is so crowded that we're lucky we've got accommodation at all. Doubly lucky, in fact,' he continued toughly, 'in that had Gillian given thought to cancel the train reservation for Edwards and Shaw, then besides me you'd have two strangers of lord knows what sex for company.' Jolene was soaking in every word when, his jaw jutting at an aggressive angle, he gritted, 'Now, if you want to make something of that—go ahead. I assure you that if I could find somewhere else to sleep this night, I would.'

Jolene felt as though she had just been chewed up and spat out again. But she had no intention whatsoever of letting him see what it did to her that he could not bear the sight of her. 'Is it just for one night?' she questioned snappily, hoping to convey that, although it went against the grain that she had to accept the situation, she could accept it much better if she did not have to put up with him for two nights.

'We're due in Novosibirsk shortly after lunch tomorrow,' Cheyne rapped back.

Realising that she had already accepted the situation for what it was, some stubbornness in her made her hold out before final capitulation. 'Couldn't Gillian book herself a separate sleeper?' she questioned. 'After all, she was the one who was supposed to be coming with you.'

'I've told you,' Cheyne began exasperatedly, 'sex, male or female, doesn't count on this...' he broke off suddenly, and his tone was marginally less harsh. 'I'm glad to see that you now believe that I've no relationship with Gillian outside the office.' His tone had toughened again, though, as he went on to refer to her question, 'But since you ask, Gillian is mature enough to take in her stride that when a train is as popular as this one, she's been extremely fortunate to get a berth at all for the date she wanted.'

'Thanks,' Jolene grunted. In contrast to Viktor's flattery, Cheyne Templeton was one insult after another. She considered that, in the light of Gillian's being 'mature' enough to take this in her stride, Cheyne had just told her to grow up. Turning her face away from him, she stared unseeing out of the half-curtained window, and wondered if she would have protested so strongly had she not loved the bossy brute.

'Besides which,' Cheyne, his tone much lighter than it had been, suddenly caused her to look away from the window and at him, 'Gillian was so taken with the idea of actually travelling on the Trans-Siberian Railway that she probably wouldn't have cared had she to share a compartment with the devil himself.'

Was he in some way apologising for his previous remark? Jolene wondered. His lighter tone seemed to suggest that he was. For about five seconds she was determined that he could go and take a running jump before she'd accept his apology. Then all at once her heartbeats were accelerating, because she just knew that Cheyne was not the kind of man who normally went around apologising for anything, which had to mean that he did like her a little after all, didn't it?

It was no good, a smile was breaking out somewhere deep in the heart of her, and that smile would not be kept in. Indeed, it became more of a grin when, her eyes wide on his, she returned as lightly, 'If you'll pardon the impertinence, I suppose it's better the devil you know than the one you don't.'

Dark grey eyes, warm dark grey eyes, were fixed on hers and she saw the corners of his mouth go up. 'Impertinence pardoned,' he drawled, and the atmosphere in the compartment all at once considerably eased. 'Drink your tea,' he instructed her.

The stout and solid door of the compartment was left open and the morning passed in a happy vein. Cheyne went out exploring once their tea had been downed, and although Jolene had a paperback she could be enjoying had she felt like reading, she was gaining more enjoyment from just being on the train.

Feeling happier within herself and starting to think that it was not so much that Cheyne could not bear the sight of her as that, with him wanting the best out of this business trip, and working hard towards that end, it was only natural he should find her fussing about the sleeping arrangements irritating.

She gazed out at the snowy landscape and felt so good about him that she was ready to forgive him every slight, real or imagined. For some time she gazed for the pleasure of it out of the train window at the white-blanketed scene with its forests and occasional village of larch-built properties. How vast Siberia was, she mused; she had some vague recollection of its being over four million square miles, and she wondered if she had got that right, for four million square miles was indeed vast.

Having investigated under the lower bunks to discover blankets and fold-away mattresses, Jolene decided to step out of the compartment. In a very few paces she was through the slid-back open door and out into the carpeted corridor where white and blue patterned curtains covered the bottom half of the window.

For some time she stood at the hand-rail which ran along the length of the corridor and gazed out at a similar scene to the one she had witnessed from the compartment.

Feeling adventurous, she walked to the end where, next to where the conductress responsible for that coach had her own quarters, was the toilet and wash-hand basin. Having inspected these facilities, Jolene returned to the corridor. She was staring in some absorption at the solid fuel-burning samovar which stood in a corner of the corridor and which was adorned with a collection of pipes, handles and valves, when Cheyne appeared from down the other end of the coach.

'Hungry?' he enquired, and looked friendly.

'I could eat a horse!' she smiled.

'You'll wish you hadn't said that,' he drawled, and suddenly she was happy again and she just had to burst out laughing. She saw his expression go serious as his eyes went to her mouth. Then that friendly look was there once more in his eyes, and with his glance back on her eyes, he said, 'Let's eat,' and led the way.

Happily Jolene followed him through train corridors. Happily she leapt on to the metal humps where each coach was connected to the next. And, with the whole of her being tingling, she held on to the hand he offered each time she leapt from the metal hump into the next coach.

The restaurant car was busy, but she and Cheyne had a table for four to themselves. There were the same blue and white patterned curtains starting half-way down the window as elsewhere on the train and, not wanting to miss any of it as they waited for their meal, Jolene pulled the curtains to one side and looked out.

The same snowbound, tree-filled scene met her eyes, with the occasional track of some wild animal in the snow. She was unaware, however, of her rapt expression until suddenly Cheyne asked quietly, 'Enjoying it?'

'It's absolutely fantastic,' she replied, and decided there and then that, given the unpropitious way this train ride had begun, she was, from that instant, going to enjoy every moment of it. Thinking that she was going to need some good experience to look back on when, back in England, long cold days would pass without her ever seeing him, Jolene found herself hurrying into speech. 'You intimated that Gillian Frampton is worth her weight in gold as a PA, but I don't think you can be such a bad boss, after all,' she told him suddenly.

'After all?' he enquired drily, with a lift of his left eyebrow.

As she was about to reply, just then a waitress came to serve them with a sliced pork and chopped spring onion starter. No sooner had the waitress gone, though, than Jolene, taking up her knife and fork, questioned, 'It was Gillian's idea to take the Trans-Siberian Express to Novosibirsk, wasn't it?'

'It was,' he conceded.

'Which makes you quite an—um—a nice employer, that you agreed.'

'Steady, Jolene!' he warned. 'You nearly fell over yourself there trying not to spread the compliments on too thick!' And as she grinned, for in truth she had hung back a little with her praise in case he thought she was purposely trying to butter him up, he drawled, 'Though would that I were worthy of your good opinion. But in point of fact, although it made no difference to me how we got to Novosibirsk, I told Gillian that only so long as she could make the arrangements to fit in with my Novosibirsk schedule could she go ahead and make the train reservations.'

In Jolene's opinion that still made him a nice employer. More, it made him a kind employer, because he could have just as easily have told her to forget it and to make arrangements for them to get there more swiftly by air.

'She must have been thrilled, anyhow,' she insisted.

Cheyne nodded. 'She was,' he had to agree. 'But she was even more thrilled to tell me on my return that she wouldn't be coming on the trip after all.'

'Because of the baby?' Jolene smiled, but did not need him to answer.

She tucked into her next course of tomato soup, happy for Gillian who, plainly because of past disappointments, had said nothing to Cheyne of her hope that she was having a baby until he returned from his other trip, by which time she was really sure.

'Not a horse in sight,' Jolene murmured when the next course of beef and a variety of chips unlike any she had ever seen before was placed in front of her.

She flicked a glance to Cheyne and saw that although his expression seemed amused, in his eyes there was a thoughtful look. It gave her the strangest impression that he had been studying her for the last couple of minutes.

That whimsical notion passed, however, and after a piece of cake and a cup of coffee they did the return—for her—hand- and body-tingling leap from coach to coach, to their own compartment.

What with pulling into a station soon afterwards, and finding things of interest from both compartment window and corridor window, it was about half an hour later that Jolene returned to take a seat in the compartment. Not many minutes later Cheyne joined her, and so began an afternoon that for Jolene was little short of magical.

On any other train journey due to take as long as this one, she would have been tempted to get out a book. But she made no attempt to read that afternoon, because she was caught up in the grip of the excitement of actually being on the Trans-Siberian Railway. And, to heighten that excitement, she and Cheyne appeared to be getting on well.

Not one single abrasive word had passed between them since they had gone to lunch and, as a bonus, it seemed that Cheyne had done sufficient exploring of the train for the moment, and was content to stay put—with her.

Intermittently they stared out of the window, passed some comment, or drew each other's attention to something a little different on the landscape.

'Two magpies—there!' Jolene suddenly directed his attention, and wanted to believe that he, like her, was storing up each and every memory, but she very much doubted it.

From time to time her interest was taken with the happenings inside the train, and she watched through the open compartment door at how the conductress would unroll a length of drugget to cover the corridor carpet whenever the train halted at a station. As soon as the disembarking passengers were off, and the embarking passengers were on, she would roll the drugget up again.

At some time during the afternoon the conductress came round with a trolley of items available for purchase. Deciding against chocolates or sweets, for she found the meals quite filling, Jolene exchanged some roubles for a pack of playing cards; only to smile with Cheyne when on inspection she discovered that the pack contained only thirty-six cards—all that were required for Russian card games, apparently. It was moments like that shared smile with him, though, which she hoarded to her like some miser.

With Jolene savouring every moment of this companionable, enchanted time with him, they spent some time in desultory easy conversation. Cheyne had just mentioned that there were two types of accommodation on the Express, and how they had been booked into the 'hard' as opposed to the 'soft' class, when the conductress came and brought them steaming glasses of tea.

'*Spahsseebah,*' Jolene thanked her, and when the conductress had gone, and sensing that Cheyne would have preferred the other class, she suggested, 'I don't suppose Gillian knew that one had a choice when she made the booking.'

'I don't suppose she did,' he murmured, but there was a warm light in his eyes when he added, 'I've known Gillian for long enough to be aware of where she excels and where she fails, Jolene, so you've no need to defend her to me. But then,' he went on, 'I've a suspicion that as well as your being outwardly beautiful, there's an inner beauty in you.' Jolene was looking at him, speechless and hardly believing her hearing, when he got to his feet, turned away from her and tossing something casually over his shoulder about stretching his legs, left the compartment.

She was still glowing from what he had said about her outer as well as her inner beauty long after he had left. Surely to have said such a thing must mean that he liked her—didn't it?

Her thoughts were still hopping here and there, with Cheyne the central pivot, when she glanced at the table, where his tea was no longer steaming. From there, however, her glance flicked to the flower vase, which she had intended to fill with water so that the rose Viktor had given her should not die. But, with startled eyes, she saw that she had no need to take any such action, because the rose which she had personally placed in that porcelain vase was no longer there!

Surprised to say the least, Jolene stared as though hypnotised at the vase that now contained only the greenery for decoration which had been there when she and Cheyne had boarded the train. Ridiculously then, her first thought was that Cheyne, having taken against Viktor for some reason, had lost no time in removing all evidence of him.

Her next thought was to realise just how ridiculous that first thought was. Cheyne would not care a tinker's cuss either way about Viktor Sekirkin. Cheyne was a businessman first, last and always. It would matter not to him whether he found Viktor agreeable or disagreeable; what did matter was that he, or members of his team, could talk engineering to the Russian.

Having seen what an idiot she was to have such wild notions, the best Jolene could come up with as an explanation for where her rose had disappeared to, was that the conductress must have removed it. Evidence that she had been in the compartment while they had been at lunch lay in the fact that freshly laundered sheets and pillow slips which had not been there before now lay on top of one of the upper bunks. Perhaps there was some railway rule which said that only greenery of a uniform nature must be placed in the vases, Jolene cogitated. Or, bearing in mind a very jerky stop the train had made once that afternoon—and bearing in mind how house-proud the conductress was with her drugget—perhaps she did not intend to risk having a passenger put water in the vase when, should the train make another jerky stop, some of the bedding might get christened.

However, Jolene remembered Cheyne telling her she had beauty, and where Viktor's rose had got to did not figure greatly in her thoughts from then on.

She was standing in the corridor staring at what looked like a timber mill as they flashed by when a movement up the corridor to her left sent her heart drumming. A second later the tall figure of Cheyne Templeton was standing next to her.

Feeling choked suddenly, but needing to say something—anything—'Your tea's gone cold,' she told him, and could have groaned aloud at the inanity of her remark. For goodness' sake, Cheyne was the sort of person who, if he had wanted a drink of tea, would have stayed and drunk it, not decided that to stretch his legs was preferable to sit tea-drinking.

He quickly sent all thoughts of what a fool she was from her mind, though, when, as easily as before, he remarked, 'Which makes it just as well that dinner is only half an hour away.'

'Really?' Jolene turned from watching the view. 'I haven't had a chance to get hungry since I've been here!' she exclaimed.

After a quick wash and tidy-up, she went with Cheyne past all the sliding doors which had previously been solidly closed but which were now open, through several coaches to the restaurant car.

Jolene was barely aware of what she tucked into that night, for Cheyne had not altered from the dear companion he had been that afternoon, and she was falling deeper and deeper in love with him all the while. More, she was growing to like him exceedingly well too.

That they had finished the first course of ham and dill pickle, and were on their second course of mashed potatoes, peas and beef, barely impinged as Cheyne kept her amused with an anecdote here and there, and listened attentively to anything that she had to say.

There was a lull in their conversation as the waitress came to their table and asked them which they would prefer, tea or coffee. They both opted for coffee, but as the waitress filled their cups and went on her way, the question of whether Gillian Frampton would be returning to her office after the birth of her baby came to her mind, and before she could think about it she had put the question to Cheyne.

'Not a chance,' he replied, and added, 'After waiting this long she's far more mother-minded than she's career-minded.' Suddenly then, though, as Jolene looked at him and felt good inside that he had so unhesitatingly answered her question, she saw him hesitate, as though in mid-thought. Then he was rubbing his forefinger along his chin as though he was thinking hard about something. And then, to her complete astonishment, he said quietly, 'Talking of careers, and not forgetting that you *are* career-minded, my PA's job will be advertised both internally as well as externally——' He paused, and then let fall, 'I'm sure any application from you would be favourably looked on.'

Jolene was still somewhere up on cloud nine as she and Cheyne made their way back to their compartment. Surely, if she had not suddenly gone dense from the shock of it, Cheyne could only have been saying that the job of his PA was hers for the asking!

Feeling thrilled and delighted at the thought of not only working for him but of seeing him every day, Jolene was still trying to take it in when, with Cheyne having taken out some paperwork and sitting opposite her, she got out her paperback and pretended to read.

For how long she sat there occasionally turning over a page but taking in nothing of the printed matter, she could not have said. Though daylight had long since gone, and it must have been some time since she had turned over a page when, with her thoughts on how Cheyne must be pleased with the work she had so far done for him, he said into the quietness of their compartment, 'Why not get into bed?'

'I've had it with this book, anyhow,' she responded, lest his suggestion stemmed from the fact that he knew she was not progressing very far with her reading.

Together they got out mattresses, blankets and pillows, and while Jolene made herself up a lower bunk Cheyne manhandled her suitcase down on to one end of the lower bunk opposite. While she extracted what she needed, he attended to making up a bed for himself on the bunk over the top of hers.

It felt strange to her to be taking her nightly wash in the swaying facilities of the train, and even stranger to be walking up the train corridor in her nightdress and dressing-gown and clutching her toilet bag. But Cheyne had said 'When in Rome', and for goodness' sake, she had been so happy that day, and from that bad start, that if he now said black was white she would have gone along with it.

For all her 'when in Rome' thoughts, though, nothing could have induced her to part with her cotton dressing-gown when, back in the compartment, she climbed into her narrow bed with it still on.

Cheyne was not yet in bed, and she guessed he would probably work on for a few more hours yet. But she watched him when, having instructed her to go to bed, he went to the sliding door, and for the first time that day, closed the solid wood compartment door on any passerby.

'Goodnight, Cheyne,' Jolene bade him, and tucking her dressing-gown closer around her, she went to lie down to get what sleep she could.

'Good...' he broke off, and looking at him, Jolene saw his expression suddenly change to one little short of incredulity when, instead of ending with the 'night' she had expected, he substituted, '...lord,' and added, 'You *are*!'

'Are what?' she asked, having no clue to what he meant.

Cheyne was still looking thunderstruck as he exclaimed, 'You really *are* a virgin.'

Startled, because that was the last thing she had expected, suddenly that old imp of mischief had awakened in her again, and, with her green eyes large and innocent, she queried, 'Would I lie to you, sir?' and, turning her back to him, but expecting at any moment to hear the wonderful sound of his laugh, she closed her eyes.

She did not hear him laugh, though, and she realised that he could not have been amused by her reply. She reached out a hand and put out the light by her head, and over the next few hours she lay listening while Cheyne rustled papers and generally moved around.

Once she drifted off into a light sleep, but when she came awake again and could not go back to sleep, she got around to thinking that she might never travel on the Trans-Siberian Railway again, and most assuredly never again with Cheyne. On that thought, she decided she wanted to stay awake through the rest of the night so that she could keep this memory, too, to take out and savour when she was back in England.

But, the laws of cussedness being what they were, no sooner had she determined to stay awake than in no time her eyelids were drooping.

The next time she awoke it was because she was jolted awake. 'What . . . !' she began as something fell over her bed.

But she was immediately reassured by Cheyne, who swiftly told her, 'Don't be alarmed, Jolene. The driver suddenly put the brakes on and . . .'

'I'm not alarmed,' she was quick to reassure him in return, realising as sleep started to go from her that he must have been out of his bunk looking out of the windows at the night sky or something when the train had come to an abrupt and unexpected stop, and had jolted him off his feet.

There followed a few seconds in which Cheyne moved from a semi-recumbent position over her to sit up. Then, when for no reason Jolene decided to sit up too, suddenly, as Cheyne went to stand, they both leaned forward at the same time, and touched—and that touch was electric!

Quite how it happened Jolene could never afterwards have said, but just the feel of Cheyne's chest against hers was enough to send wild yearning surging through her. Who reached for whom she neither knew nor cared; all she knew in those moments of Cheyne's arms coming round her, and her arms going around him, was that in his arms was where she wanted to be—and that it seemed so right.

Then Cheyne's mouth was over hers, his lips parting her lips, and as he held her firmly to him and kissed her, willingly Jolene returned his kiss. Then again and again he kissed her, and she never wanted him to stop.

'Oh, Jolene!' he cried once, and the next moment he was pushing her back against her mattress, and moving her bed covers away in order to get closer to her.

'Oh, Cheyne,' she breathed, and gloried in this closeness, as his hands caressed her shoulders and her back, then with his hands on her hips he half lay with her, pulling her yet closer to him. 'Cheyne!' she breathed again as a fire shot to life in her and he awakened feelings in her that were totally new.

His body was warm against hers, and she wanted to know more of him. And it was as if he was aware of how she felt, for suddenly he was untying the belt of her robe and pushing the folds of the cotton aside.

Again she wanted to call his name, and she was not sure, as his hands caressed her breasts and she clutched convulsively at him, that his name did not leave her on a moan of wanting.

But if she wanted him, then Cheyne telling her, 'Sweet Jolene, I want you,' was all she needed to hear. A groan escaped him when his body moved against hers, and she arched her body to get nearer still.

The masculine feel of him as he pressed down on her was exquisite torment, and when his warm, seeking fingers moved the shoulder-straps of her nightdress to one side, and his mouth traced tiny kisses over her naked breasts, she began to tremble.

Tormented beyond enduring when his kisses on her breasts were mingled with tantalising fingers which gently caressed her swollen globes and the throbbing peaks he had created, Jolene again cried out his name.

Then several things happened all at once, and all within the next couple of seconds, it was ended. For in the same moment of Cheyne huskily groaning, 'Joley, sweet, sweet virgin!' the train—which she later realised had been standing in a station—suddenly jerked into life. And in that instant Cheyne's words suddenly reminded her of that other man who had wanted to take her virginity, and she momentarily panicked. In her panic she was not certain that she did not hear Cheyne croak hoarsely, 'Oh—my stars!' because panic was making her deaf, and she was pushing him away from her.

She afterwards realised that she must have gained extra strength from somewhere, for suddenly Cheyne had left her. And all in one movement, or so it seemed to her distressed eyes, he had left her, found the door handle in the light from the station, and swiftly, before she could call him back, he had put himself on the other side of the door.

CHAPTER EIGHT

THERE had been no chance of Jolene going back to sleep after Cheyne had so hurriedly left the compartment, but with the coming of daylight common sense began to rear its ugly head, and she was never more glad that she had not called him back.

He had not returned since he had left in the dark hours, and she had no way of knowing where he was. But when at about six-thirty she left her bunk, took some fresh clothing from her case, and grabbed hold of her toilet bag, far from wanting to know where he was, Jolene was wishing she might never have to see him again.

See him again, though, she did, and before she was ready, too. Because as she slid back the compartment door and took a step into the corridor, Cheyne turned from the rail where he had been watching the landscape go by, and, his face unsmiling, he looked at her gravely.

With her face suddenly aflame with colour, Jolene turned a speedy sharp right away from him and headed blindly for the small stainless steel compartment at the end of the coach.

Locking herself in, she methodically set about getting washed and dressed, but the whole while her thoughts were going off at a tangent. She still loved him, she knew that for a fact—her quick glance at him before she had spun away had shown her that. She had felt a softness, a gentleness in her for him. He had been dressed in what appeared to be pyjama bottoms and, from the brief

139

glimpse she saw through the openings of his short robe, no pyjama top. With a dark stubble on his chin, he seemed more endearing than he had ever been.

Whether he would have said anything to her, had she given him half a chance, she had left it too late to find out. What she had found out, though, was that she was regretting, more than she had regretted anything in her life, that she had for a moment responded to him so eagerly—not only those few short hours ago, but back at Lake Baikal.

Wondering where her natural reserve had gone when it came to giving displays of affection, Jolene realised that, loving Cheyne the way she did, her reserve hadn't stood a chance up against him and his expertise. What would have happened had she not panicked momentarily she could only guess at, but she thanked her lucky stars that she had panicked and thrust him away from her. Plainly, he was another who had a 'penchant for virgins', though seeing that she must have represented some sort of a challenge to him, it puzzled her briefly why he had left the compartment so entirely without argument.

A moment later Jolene had decided that Cheyne Templeton did not like things made too easy. As she'd suspected, he liked a challenge. Quite clearly, he was prepared to bide his time. With something of a shock, Jolene at that point suddenly had to give credence to the thought that his only reason for offering her Gillian Frampton's job when she left to have her baby was his intention to, at some future time, have one Jolene Draper in his bed.

She was ready to go back to the compartment, though, when all at once it occurred to her that she had better keep a guard on her tongue. For, feeling mentally battered and bruised and as though she had just been through the wringer, she suddenly realised that, with his astuteness, any unthought word of hurt from her could give him something to think about.

Jolene left the small room at the end of the corridor knowing that her pride would never survive should Cheyne glean so much as half an idea of how desperately in love with him she was.

Her heart did a wayward flip, nevertheless, when she saw that, although he was now trousers- and shirt-clad, Cheyne was standing by that same rail as though he had never moved.

By the time she reached him, however, she had herself under the strictest control. This time, too, she had no intention of doing a disappearing act before giving him a chance to say anything he intended to.

To her mind, though, his manner, for one who she had just reasoned was determined to have her in his bed at some future time, was a bit on the casual side when he found the energy to enquire, 'Everything all right?'

'Fine,' she smiled at him brightly. And whether he was enquiring after her welfare or—as she spotted the leather wash bag in his hand—the ablutions, 'The water's lovely and hot,' she told him, and then, as casual as he, she strolled into their compartment.

Looking around, she saw that he had been busy stowing away mattresses and blankets and generally making the compartment look less like a bedroom. She did not thank him for attending to her bedding for her— to her way of thinking, there was something very final about his actions.

With nothing left for her to do but to return her things to her suitcase and strap it up ready for when they reached Novosibirsk, Jolene was soon finished and with plenty of time left in which to think. She was aware that she was probably over-sensitive where Cheyne was concerned, but, bearing in mind how she had thought there was something very final about his actions, notwithstanding his casual tone just now, she could not help wondering, had she really got it right? Did Cheyne still want her in his bed? Or was it that maybe that had been the case, but he had now gone off the idea?

The latter seemed to be very much more likely, she discovered. For the next time she saw him he was clean-shaven, had his leather wash-bag under one arm, and two glasses of tea in their metal holders in his hands.

'Tea up,' he said easily, and in a tone even a person with the most vivid imagination could not have called amorous.

'Thanks,' she replied in friendly vein, and while she composed herself to make affable conversation he set down the tea on the table, and stowed his wash-bag away. Then, just to show how much he was panting after her, he picked up one of the glasses of tea and took it with him out into the corridor. The view, that had changed little over the miles, had far more appeal for him, apparently, than she had.

When Cheyne came to tell her casually that it was time to go to breakfast, Jolene had done enough thinking to be heartily glad that she had suffered that moment of panic that had caused her to push him from her. Because it was painfully clear that he would have acted just as casually to her now, had she given herself to him—their lovemaking would have meant nothing to him.

She was much relieved too, as they went from coach to coach, that today, unlike yesterday, he appeared to think her fleet enough of foot not to come to grief if he did not offer her a steadying hand. Jolene was past thanking him for anything when he waited but a step away as though to be on hand should his 'steadying hand' services become necessary.

All of which made it most surprising to her that when she was going through a real hate session against him, she could, for pride's sake, make a pleasant remark as they sat down at their table. 'This dark-coloured bread's delicious, isn't it?' she smiled, and then, for all the world as if she was starving, though she felt as though any crumb she chewed might choke her, she took hold of a piece of bread and buttered it, then reached for some cheese to go with it.

When after breakfast she returned to the compartment, she caught hold of her paperback as though nothing would do but that she must finish it before they got off the train. By then it did not surprise her that Cheyne had found some other part of the train to hold some interest for him. Her only surprise was that when lunchtime arrived he remembered her for long enough to come and tell her, 'We'll have lunch now, Jolene,' and his manner was as easy as before when she looked up. 'I've someone to see this afternoon—there may not be a chance to snatch a bite again before dinner.'

Having scotched any disclaimer that she was hungry before she could make it, Jolene could do nothing but smile, and give the general impression that she couldn't wait to start eating.

Curiosity, however, began to stir in her so that, when once more seated in the restaurant, she thought she would be on fairly safe ground if any topic of conversation she entered into centred solely on work. 'Shall I need my notepad this afternoon?' she enquired as, knife and fork in hand, she prepared to tackle her starter.

'Notepad?' queried Cheyne, and realising what she was talking about, 'Oh, I shan't need you this afternoon,' he told her blandly. 'Lyuda and I will be able to manage quite well, I'm sure.' Gripping her knife and fork as if they were some life-support machine, as for the first time in her life jealousy struck, Jolene was damned if she would ask him who Lyuda was. To her chagrin, Cheyne did not offer to enlighten her either, but with a cool smile he told her, 'You can have the afternoon off.'

About to give him a snappy 'Gee, thanks', Jolene checked to remind herself that she must not give him the tiniest clue to the hurt she was feeling inside. 'Lovely,' she said, and even had a smile on her face as she told him, 'A Saturday afternoon in Novosibirsk has to be different from a Saturday afternoon at home. Now...'

'And what would Jolene Draper be doing on a Saturday afternoon back in England?' Cheyne interrupted her as though on impulse and as though he was really interested.

But Jolene had seen sufficient of his *lack* of interest that morning to know that this show of interest was not sincere. Though, since he seemed to be doing his best to get things back to normal after giving in to his masculine urges during the early hours, she made an effort to answer him just as though she truly believed he was hanging on to her every word with bated breath.

'At this time of year, I'd probably be trying to do something in the garden to clear up the ravages of winter,' she replied, and discovered that she had not fully bored him out of his skull when he came back,

'You help your father in his garden?'

She shook her head. 'I've my own garden,' she told him, and explained, 'I don't live at home. I inherited my grandmother's bungalow when she died, and decided, rather than sell it, to move in.'

'Alone?' he questioned abruptly, and realising that she *had* been boring him to death, she answered abruptly, though possibly more snappily than abruptly, when she tossed back,

'The men I know always have to go home to their wives at night!'

Cheyne threw her an acerbic look. It signalled the end of his making any attempt to get matters back to normal between them.

Jolene told herself that she did not give a hoot anyway as they returned to their compartment. The thrill for her had disappeared. The excitement of this Russian trip had gone. As far as she was concerned, she would far rather be going home this Saturday than next. Roll on next Saturday, was the best she could wish for as the train pulled into Novosibirsk.

She was of the opinion, as she and Cheyne alighted, that nothing could happen to make her feel more down than she was feeling just then. She had reckoned, however, without a most attractive-looking woman of about thirty who at that instant suddenly spotted them and came and launched herself at her tall employer.

'Cheyne—darlink!' she trilled, and as Jolene looked on with jealousy turning a knife, Cheyne and the woman made a meal—so Jolene thought—of kissing each other on both cheeks.

Thoroughly fed up suddenly, Jolene's spirits were not lifted at all when Cheyne all at once seemed to remember that he had a secretary somewhere—albeit only an acting secretary—and brought the attractive-looking woman over to her. 'Jolene, I'd like you to meet Lyudmila Antipova,' he smiled. 'Lyuda,' he said, and while Jolene was rebelliously thinking it no wonder that he'd said 'I shan't need you' and was certain herself that they would manage *quite well* without her, Cheyne completed the introduction.

Lyudmila Antipova went with them to their hotel, and from what Jolene could make out she was some sort of floating liaison officer connected with the conference which was to begin on Monday. It was apparently her lot to help to see to it that the conference ran smoothly, and to time. She and Cheyne were to spend the afternoon together, with Lyudmila Antipova giving him a rundown of the conference schedule and dealing with any queries he might have. To Jolene's mind, Lyudmila Antipova enjoyed her work.

Feeling decidedly out of sorts, Jolene took herself off for a walk around the locality as soon as the formalities of checking into their hotel were completed. She was glad to have the afternoon off, she told herself determinedly as she found herself in Red Avenue and looked about. She hoped both Lyudmila Antipova and 'Cheyne—darlink' enjoyed their 'business' afternoon.

Jealousy, she realised as she crossed the wide, wide avenue to study a giant statue of Lenin, was truly a dreadful scourge. She left her contemplation of the statue and recrossed the wide avenue by subway, and tried to rid herself of her jealousy.

She went into a bookshop and was having an idle look round when, attempting to think logically, she saw that there was no logic to love—or jealousy. Had she not been so painfully caught up in both, she realised, she would have quite liked the attractive and friendly Lyudmila Antipova.

Like her or not, Jolene was to see a lot of the Russian woman over the next few days. She dined with them that night, and the next day she arranged a visit to Akademgorodok, where they toured an institute of Geology and Geophysics. But while Cheyne showed a deep interest in the various samples of minerals on display, Jolene's eyes were drawn again and again to the large map of the USSR on the wall, and to the crescent-shaped Lake Baikal. She had been happy there.

By the time Monday morning arrived she was still doing her utmost not to show by word or look how she felt about Cheyne. She was aware by then, though, that an air of strain was there between them. She did not think it was just her imagination, either. For although in front of Lyuda, as she too now called her, he was always unfailingly polite, no sooner were they on their own than his words to her would be clipped and verging more on the hostile than the polite.

She supposed she must be grateful that the times she saw him alone without Lyuda being there were very few. Indeed, Lyuda was even there with them at breakfast that Monday morning, and leaving nothing to chance, apparently, as she breezed in, sat down with them, and declared, 'I have decided, Cheyne, that as you are so special, I will come with you to take you to the conference centre.'

Jolene saw his mouth curve upwards, and jealousy took another stab at her. It seemed light years since she herself had been able to bring that look of being amused to his face. She kept her expression bland, however, when, with Lyuda under some strain too that morning, it seemed, Cheyne saw through her remark and commented lightly, 'You decided, if I'm not mistaken, Lyuda, that rather than risk my getting to the conference late, you'd come and make sure I'd be on time.'

Lyuda gave a shout of laughter, and abruptly turned from him. 'You like the blinis, Jolene?' she asked, observing her spooning some sour cream on to a most palatable pancake.

'They're scrumptious,' Jolene told her.

'Scrumptious—this is a new word for me,' Lyuda told her, and Jolene spent a few minutes explaining the word. Then Lyuda was anxiously looking at her watch, and as if to put her out of her anxiety Cheyne told her they would see about getting on their way now.

Stepping from the car at the modern conference centre, Jolene could not help but swallow emotionally when, on going up the concrete steps towards the entrance, she saw the large sign, written in English, that read, 'International Conference on Worldwide Economic Development'. Cheyne, her Cheyne, the man she loved, and was in love with, had been invited to speak to this international gathering, and whose heart could help but burst with pride? Even though she knew that Cheyne was not really her Cheyne, nothing could take away that feeling of pride.

Throughout that Monday she tried to behave as she thought Gillian Frampton would, and took down in shorthand anything she thought would be of interest or needed for future reference. The result was, though, that she took down far too much shorthand and was working way past midnight that night to get it all typed back.

She consoled herself that she had just had as good as a five-day break from her typewriter, and told herself that she was here to work anyway. And, having recharged her batteries with a few hours' sleep, she was pencil poised and willing when on Tuesday morning she again took her seat at the conference.

Her insides became knotted up with nerves when the afternoon arrived and Cheyne descended from the auditorium and on to the stage to deliver his speech. Yet, with so many hundreds there to listen to him, she could not see any sign of nervousness about him at all.

Her pride in him seemed out of all bounds as he began to speak. She was monumentally proud of him then—to the point of tears. Proud of him, and proud to be a part of his team. To her mind, and she admitted that she was biased, Cheyne's speech was the best of the lot. He spoke clearly and concisely, got his point across, and then, when the title of his subject seemed anything but humorous, he had his audience laughing at some comical reference he had thrown in.

Jolene's only regret as back in the hotel that night she typed back all that she had taken down was that she had been so engrossed in seeing him tall, relaxed and in command of not only his theme but his audience that she had not written down one word of his speech.

They left Novosibirsk the next day, and Lyuda came to the airport to see them off. 'Goodbye, Jolene,' she bade her, and shook hands with her enthusiastically. Then she was turning to Cheyne. 'I shall see you again,' she told him, and when to Jolene's eyes he seemed to enjoy it rather than object to it, Lyuda went into her cheek-kissing routine.

'I hope so,' he smiled, and as they parted from Lyuda Jolene was set to wonder whether he hoped to see her again because of his other business interests, or the present joint business venture he was hoping to negotiate with her countrymen, or because it was Lyuda personally he was hoping to see again.

Being in love, Jolene thought, as the plane took off for Leningrad, was hell.

It was a four-hour flight from Novosibirsk to Leningrad, but because of the hour time-change from Irkutsk to Novosibirsk, and the four-hour time-change from Novosibirsk to Leningrad, they arrived in that city at the same time at which they had taken off.

They checked into the Hotel Leningrad, and were in the middle of a late lunch when Cheyne told her, 'We're meeting a Mr Novikov at three-thirty, so you'd better be ready at three.'

'We're meeting him in the hotel or at his office?' Jolene queried, wanting, if they were going out, to be already dressed in her top coat at three rather than be late for the appointment by going back to her room for it.

'It'll hardly take you half an hour to get from your room to the ground floor!' Cheyne told her shortly, and as Jolene swallowed down a snappy retort, she wondered how it was that she could at one and the same time look at him and love him with all her being yet in that same moment want to give him a punch on that oh, so aggressive jaw.

At five to three she was down in the ground floor lobby with her hat and coat on. At two minutes to three precisely, Cheyne joined her. Without a word to each other they went to keep the appointment.

Vladimir Novikov was a sombre-looking man who, Jolene gathered, worked on a sort of Board of Trade end of things. His secretary Natasha was there too, and from what went on at that meeting it seemed that Mr Novikov was very keen for the joint venture to go ahead. He was more jovial than sombre, at any rate, when at the end of a long meeting they shook hands all round, and she and Cheyne returned to their hotel.

'I've just time to give you some dictation before dinner,' Cheyne told her as the lift stopped at their floor, and they stepped out into the lounge area. 'I'll meet you here in five minutes,' he told her as they went to collect their room keys from the floor attendant.

Jolene took dictation before dinner, ate dinner with barely a word passing between her and Cheyne, and got away from him as soon as she could to go back to her room and again type until past midnight.

When she eventually climbed into bed, it was to recall, sadly, how that morning they had been in Siberia, but were no longer there. How Siberia had been magical for her, but how, now, all she wanted to do was to go home.

After breakfast the next morning she went to Cheyne's room and handed him the pages and pages of neat typing she had completed. But when not so much as a thank-you did she get, she really did want to hit him.

It was touch and go then that she did not fire up with something sarcastic such as 'Don't mention it—it was a pleasure'. Somehow, though, she bit back the tart words, and when he stood at the door of his room looking tough and as if to ask what was she hanging around for, she questioned, 'Do you want me for anything?' not very agreeably, she had to admit.

She felt more as though he had hit her than wanting to hit him again, when, raising one eyebrow aloft, 'Nothing,' he told her sarcastically, 'that I can think of.' Abruptly she turned away, and had taken a couple of brisk paces from him before he called, 'Jolene!' Go to hell, she thought, and with tears in her eyes she kept on walking.

She determined half an hour later that she had had enough of being at his beck and call. So far as she knew, and half an hour ago he had more or less confirmed it, there was nothing more on the agenda for that day other than to catch a flight to Moscow at some time in the early evening.

Donning her hat and coat, Jolene went out into the Leningrad streets, noticed that a thaw seemed to have set in, and hailed a taxi. She was taking the day off—she hoped Cheyne dismissed her for it.

In rebellious mood she told the taxi driver to drop her off in the shopping area, but he could have dropped her off anywhere for all the attention she was paying. By heaven, had she got it wrong to think for even an instant that Cheyne might be prepared to bide his time before he again made an attempt to seduce her! It did not need two guesses to know that when it came to biding one's time, she could bide hers forever and a day before he would want to try anything like that again. From what she could see of it, it seemed to her that, far from his having a penchant for virgins, her inexperience had put Cheyne right off.

Her head was still full of him when the taxi driver set her down in Nevsky Prospekt. She thought she had forgotten Cheyne a little while later when she made her way inside an extensive store which went by the name of The Merchants' Yard, and mingled with the jostling throng. But Cheyne was to enter her mind instantly when she came to a section selling framed pictures. For there before her, to at once transport her back to that happy time at the beautiful village of St Nicholas, was a black and white picture with a trace of grey and brown, which she felt had captured the very soul of the place. It was a large picture showing forested hills in the background, with wooden-built snow-topped bungalows and picket fences scattered in the foreground. And there in the middle, to make her feel so dreadfully sentimental that she had to draw on all her powers of self-control, was a wide snowy path that looked every bit as though it led up to the village church.

Her eyes misty, Jolene knew only that she must have this painting that seemed a mirror image of that very special village. How she was going to get the large glass-fronted, alloy-framed picture home was the least of her worries as she found an assistant, and while the assistant wrapped the picture in stout brown wrapping, she went to pay for it. It was unthinkable that she leave the picture behind.

Jolene saw Cheyne eyeing her large, flat, square, brown-paper-covered parcel which she would not let go of as their luggage was loaded into a taxi at seven o'clock that evening.

The painting, she admitted, as they checked in at the airport, was something of a liability in that she preferred to take it with her as cabin luggage. But she was in no way regretting her purchase, and still considered it unthinkable to go home without her picture when—more ordering than offering, in her view—Cheyne stated, 'I'll carry that.'

'I can manage,' she told him stiffly, and when he grunted some sort of couldn't-care-less reply, she knew that the hour-long flight to Moscow was not going to be filled with friendly conversation.

Friendliness awaited her in Moscow, however. For when they landed after a strained flight, it had just gone eleven that night when as she and Cheyne were making their way out of the airport building, they saw that Keith Shaw and Alec Edwards had come to meet them.

'Jo-Jo!' grinned Keith, having taken to her family nickname, as he kissed her cheek and gave her a hug. 'How's it going?'

'Terrific,' she smiled broadly back, and stayed smiling
even when she caught Cheyne glowering at her. Something, she gathered, had upset him. Then she forgot him
for a few moments, for Alec, having first greeted his
employer, was turning to her and was saluting her cheek
in the same manner as Keith.

Because Cheyne wanted a run-down on how the engineers had got on in Irkutsk, Jolene sat in the front of
the taxi on the way to their hotel while the others sat in
the back talking technical problems encountered and
overcome, and progress made.

Once at the hotel, however, Keith mooted that there
must be a bar open somewhere, and suggested that
perhaps all four of them could go. To her surprise,
though, not to say astonishment, she heard Cheyne,
while not intending to deprive himself of a drink, accepting the suggestion as a good idea on his own behalf,
but actually turning down the invitation on her behalf.

'Jolene's had a busy day,' he said, when she had not
at all. 'She'll want to get to bed so as to be fresh for our
meeting in the morning. Isn't that so?' he turned to her
to enquire.

As she looked into his dark grey eyes, the hot rebellious words, 'No, it jolly well isn't!' rose to her lips.
Suddenly she noticed the steely glint in his eyes, and the
rebellion in her unexpectedly died. All at once, as she
looked into those steel-cold eyes, she was hurting inside
that, all too obviously, Cheyne did not want her with
them.

'A girl needs her beauty sleep,' she took her eyes from
him to quip.

'Not in your case, Jo-Jo.' Keith earned himself a
laughing smile of reward for applying a small salve to
her hurt.

Jolene went up to her room, fixing it firmly in her head that she had not wanted to go for a boring old drink with them anyhow. What were they going to talk about but boring old engineering anyway?

Friday was an action-packed day for Jolene. It started with her sitting in on a meeting which included the Russians they had discussed the proposed venture with when they had first arrived in the USSR. Her afternoon was filled with trying to keep up with her employer, when, as if his head were teeming with a million and one things, he gave her rapid-fire dictation as though wanting to clear his head of everything. She spent the evening typing.

Saturday dawned bright and beautiful. 'Home today,' Alec said happily, their work in Russia done for the time being, and his homing instincts to see his wife and family growing stronger all the time.

'We've got a few hours to fill in first, though,' Keith answered him. 'Our plane doesn't go until half past five. We've ample time to take another look round Red Square,' he stated, and turning to Jolene, 'Fancy coming with us, Jo-Jo? We could take a look at St Basil's Cathedral, and Gums, the enormous store, is not to be missed.'

'I'd love to!' Jolene declared promptly, only to be surprised again by her employer, when he once more prevented her from taking up an invitation from Keith.

'I'm sorry, Jolene,' he cut in smoothly, to her ears not sounding sorry at all. And, when she knew that her work in Russia too was fully completed, 'I've promised to leave a report for collection. If we start now, you should be finished in time to leave it at the desk before we go.'

She realised that her work was not 'fully completed' after all, and there was nothing she could do but go with her employer after breakfast, and take down the most tedious mile of dictation about some piece of machinery which she had ever taken in her life.

She typed it back hoping that the Russian for whom it was intended could make more sense out of it than she could, for even though she read it through a couple of times, she could still not make out what the machine was supposed to do.

With half an hour to spare before they left for the airport, she put the typed pages neatly together, then went to take them to Cheyne.

'As requested,' she said when, so dear to her, he opened his door.

'Thanks,' he said coolly, although suddenly, as she looked in his eyes, Jolene thought his eyes were anything but cool, and she had the most urgent feeling then that he was about to tell her something of great importance. Indeed, it even seemed to her in the corridor lighting that a dull flush was creeping up under his skin, and suddenly her heart was pounding in the most crazy fashion. She thought he moved half a pace towards her, and then, as she grew taut with tension, the floor attendant walked by—and Jolene knew she had imagined the whole of it, as all Cheyne had to add of such 'great importance' was an equally cool, 'You'd better take charge of your passport,' and after a second or two spent back in his room he returned to the door to hand it to her.

All the way on that flight back to England Jolene upbraided herself. While owning that falling in love seemed to have removed some of her natural intelligence, she was feeling quite alarmed inside that she had imagined

Cheyne had been about to confide something of great importance, purely because she had wanted to imagine it.

She was still inwardly disquieted when the plane landed in England. Because, surely, to have started reading nonsense things in just a suspected—but probably imaginary—warm look in his eyes must mean that she was not safe left alone with him.

'That picture must be a Van Gogh at least, the way you've been lugging it everywhere with you,' Alec teased as they cleared Customs.

'It's a Rubens, actually,' she laughed, but she was crying inside. For instinct was telling her that she would be wise never to see Cheyne again, and she knew she was going to have to act on that instinct. Not that he looked as though it would break his heart to say a permanent goodbye to her.

From what she could see, he was looking heartily relieved to be back in England where, their mission over, he could concentrate on his next project.

'Miss Frampton will have arranged transport for you,' she heard him confidently telling Alec, as they made their way to the outside of the building. But when, as if right on cue, Frank, the company chauffeur Jolene had met before, drew up in one of the company cars, Cheyne surprised her by swinging round to her. 'I've my car here, I'll give you a lift,' he told her abruptly, and added as an afterthought as he cast his eye over the trolley-load of luggage, 'The three of you and your chattels will be a mite crowded in one car.'

'I shan't take up much room,' she told him quickly, and, afraid that her weak longing to spend some more time with him might yet see her giving in, she swiftly took her flight bag, portable typewriter, and her brown paper-wrapped picture to the offside of the company car.

'Suit yourself,' he shrugged, and showed how badly he wanted to give her a lift home by turning to have a few last-minute words with Alec Edwards.

Knowing herself immediately forgotten, Jolene was too proud to so much as glance his way again. Stubbornly she refused to take part in the general handshaking that went on. It hurt that Cheyne could so easily forget her, and as the car dropped off first Keith and then Alec, she wished she could so immediately forget Cheyne.

Having bade an affectionate farewell to the two engineers and with Frank ready to talk but, taking his cue from her that she wanted to be quiet, concentrating instead on his driving, Jolene went through a silent hell of knowing what she should do, but wanting with all she had not to do it.

By the time Frank was pulling up outside her bungalow, she had found, lost, and found again some of the will she needed to set out on that long tortuous road to forgetting him.

'Can I leave the typewriter for you to take in for me?' she asked Frank with a smile. 'It will save me...'

'With pleasure, Miss Draper,' he agreed cheerfully as her voice faded.

Jolene knew when she awakened on Sunday morning that she was not going to return to Templeton's to work. She probably did not have a job to go back to anyway, she mused glumly. She had only been filling in for Mr Hutton's secretary anyway, and she must be back from her sick leave by now. And if she was not, then someone in the efficient personnel department would have found Mr Hutton another temporary secretary to fill her place.

Her thoughts went from there to how one temporary secretary's job for her had been replaced by another. With warmth in her heart her eyes lit on the picture she had last night unpacked from its brown paper wrapping. As she looked at the picture, memories flooded in of Lake Baikal, Listvyanka, the village of St Nicholas and her happiness there when she had been temporary secretary to Cheyne.

She tore herself away from her beautiful memories to become aware that Cheyne would probably never realise she had even left his firm. He had his neatly typed reports—tomorrow Frank would return the portable typewriter to the company stores—and with everything in such apple-pie order, why should Cheyne Templeton remember her?

Determined to shut him out of her mind, Jolene sent her thoughts along the path of using next week to find herself another job, and of embarking on a career that would take her to the top. Within two minutes, however, she was remembering how Cheyne had as good as offered her the job of his PA when Gillian Frampton left. Promotion did not come better than that, Jolene considered, and as his PA, how much higher was there?

Realising that he was in her head again, she determinedly pushed him, and his offer of promotion, from her mind and went to telephone her parents to tell them she was home again.

Monday dawned dull and dismal and just about summed up Jolene's mood. At first she kept eyeing the clock, knowing that there was still time for her to go to work. When nine o'clock came and went, she was overcome with such an inner restlessness that she grabbed a shopping basket and went up to the village's general store.

She was back in her bungalow at a quarter to ten. Putting her fresh provisions away, she searched through the small toolkit she had inherited from her grandmother. Then, armed with the picture-hooks she had just purchased, and a hammer from the toolbox, she went to her sitting-room.

By ten o'clock the hammer was back in the toolbox, and Jolene had just returned to her sitting-room and was standing solemn-faced looking at the newly hung picture which meant so much to her, when someone rang the doorbell.

Leaving her contemplation of her picture for a while, she went to the front door and pulled it open—then very nearly fainted with shock. For, entirely unexpected, so that she had not so much as suspected that he might call, stood tall, dark-haired, dark grey-eyed and extremely grim-faced Cheyne Templeton!

His tone, when he spoke, was equally grim—though harsh described it better when, as if intent on drawing her fire, he barked, 'What the devil's the matter with you?'

Jolene opened her mouth, then closed it, then went swiftly from being totally stuck for words on seeing him standing there so unexpectedly, to being stung into retaliating hotly and sharply, 'Absolutely nothing!'

'Then why the hell aren't you at work?' he snarled.

CHAPTER NINE

REELING with shock, Jolene somehow managed to remain vertical and to appear as if she saw nothing untoward in opening her front door to find Cheyne Templeton standing there. She had some vague notion of hoping recently that he might dismiss her, but as his words 'Then why the hell aren't you at work?' played back in her mind, she realised that she still had a job—if she wanted it.

They were still standing at the door, when quite plainly his temper was burning on a short fuse. Cheyne did not wait for her reply, but said toughly, 'I thought you were interested in a career!'

'I am,' she again found her voice to reply, but, as the implication of what he was saying suddenly hit her, she grew hurt—and angry, and was all at once erupting, 'But I'm not interested in career promotion through the bedroom, th...'

'Who the hell offered you promotion that way?' he sliced through what she was saying to bark.

'Aren't *you*?' she slammed back. She was well aware that just seeing him had scattered her brain power. But with what brain-power she had remaining she could not see—since he had made a deliberate mention of her 'career', and since all her typing was already in his possession—why else he had called at her home.

'Hell's teeth!' he exploded angrily. 'You think the company got where it is today through promoting secretaries to executive status via my bed? What the hell sort of cheapjack outfit do you think I run?' he demanded harshly.

Almost Jolene apologised. Shot down in flames, she knew, as she supposed she had always known, that Cheyne ran his company with more professionalism than that. But, feeling stung that he was letting go at her on *her own doorstep*, she knew something in her would not let her apologise. 'What about—er—Tony Welsh?' she pulled out of a weak nowhere. 'He was definitely...' she broke off. 'Though I forget,' she resumed, 'you never did believe I was speaking the truth when I told you I did nothing to encourage him. You never...'

'Of course I believed you!' Cheyne chopped her off, and when she looked as though she was going to argue heatedly that this was news to her, 'Are you going to keep me standing out here all day?' he queried suddenly.

All day! By the sound of it, Jolene thought a trifle sourly, he had not called simply because he was passing. 'Come in,' she invited, before she had time to consider that maybe it would be better for him to say why he had called from where he was. With him on the outside of her home, she felt better able to cope—having invited him in, she belatedly realised that she had to afford him some sort of courtesy.

'Take a seat,' she offered as he followed her into her sitting-room. She determined, though, that her courtesy need not extend so far as to offer him a cup of coffee.

Having invited him in at all, however, even if that invitation had been forced from her, Jolene became aware, too late, just how little brain-power seeing Cheyne had left her with. For had she been thinking more clearly, and having invited him in at all, she would then have taken him to the dining-room or even the kitchen, to have him say what he had called for. Because suddenly she became aware of how still he was all at once and as she flicked a glance around her neat and tidy sitting-room, her eyes came to an abrupt stop at precisely the same spot as his.

'So that's the "Rubens" you toted all the way from Leningrad,' Cheyne commented quietly, eyeing her newly hung picture on the wall.

'As Rubens go, it's not one of his best,' she attempted to comment lightly.

'But one which obviously means something to you,' he replied, bringing his eyes away from the picture.

As Jolene saw it, since Cheyne was not going to know in a million years just how much the picture meant to her, there was nothing for it but to get him off the subject. 'Do take a seat, Cheyne,' she said, and could have bitten off her tongue for using his first name, which had just slipped out. To her relief, however, he moved to one of the easy chairs in the room. But as she fought to look quite relaxed and went and sat in an easy chair too, she saw that his eyes had gone again to the picture. 'So how was it you decided all at once that I hadn't been leading Tony Welsh on?' she asked quickly.

She felt relieved again when Cheyne took his eyes from the painting. Though she was not at all sure how she felt when he replied, 'With women like you, Jolene, men don't look for encouragement.'

'Thanks!' she said shortly, just to be on the safe side.

'Don't be offended,' he said evenly. 'I merely meant that men are attracted to you without encouragement.'

'Is that a fact?' she queried offhandedly, not sure that she believed that was any better.

She was somewhat shaken, however, when Cheyne, after looking steadily at her for a few moments, in a very deliberate kind of way said quietly, 'If you want a case in point—look at me.'

'You?' she questioned warily.

'Me,' he confirmed, and went on to stun her totally when he added, 'I've been very much aware of you, from the moment I saw you fending off Welsh's advances in the corridor that day.'

'You—have?' she choked with what breath she could find.

Cheyne nodded as he told her, 'Without any encouragement from you, I grew even more aware of you during the two subsequent interviews I had with you in my office. Never had I seen such angry green eyes,' he murmured.

'I...' Jolene tried, failed miserably, but really thought she ought to be doing something to get herself together. 'You'll forgive me if I didn't notice quite how "aware" of me you were,' she found some strength to say waspishly. 'From where I was sitting it looked very much as though you were more interested in calling me a liar than...'

'When did I ever call you a liar?' Cheyne interrupted, his tone changing abruptly to be sharp and challenging.

'You checked me out—you told me you had!' she reminded him heatedly.

'I also told you that there was a lot riding on the Russian trip. See it from my side,' he asked of her. 'You'd told me that none of what I'd seen was your fault, but from where I saw it you could well be some man-mad nymphomaniac. With the Russian expedition being so important, I couldn't afford to give you the benefit of the doubt without first making a few enquiries about you.'

'You heard about Tony Welsh's wife coming to the building before I told you,' Jolene stated, in fairness, having to go along with him when she looked at the situation from his point of view.

'From what I heard, she didn't bother to keep her voice down,' Cheyne replied.

'But, having heard that I might be a marriage breaker, you still gave me the benefit of the doubt.'

'When you explained how it was, I found I wanted to believe you,' he admitted, and for a brief few seconds Jolene floated on air.

She came down to earth all too soon, however, when, prodded by her memory, she quickly reminded him, 'You may have given me the benefit of the doubt, but that didn't prevent you from warning me off Alec and Keith when, at Heathrow, you made a point of letting me know that they were both married.'

'I can't deny it,' he owned, but a warm look had come into his dark grey eyes when he in turn remembered, 'That was when, if I hadn't realised it before, you showed me that you weren't going to be sat on by anyone. I knew I was going to have trouble with you from the moment you impudently told me that some woman had had a lucky escape in relation to my being a bachelor.'

'I was talking more to myself than to you.' Jolene thought she should mention, the warm look in his eyes causing her heart to give a small energetic burst. Then the other thing he had just said suddenly clicked, and she exclaimed, 'Trouble? Wh...'

'It was touch and go that I didn't tell you there and then that I could manage without you,' Cheyne cut in to inform her.

'At that late stage?'

'I didn't know then,' he said slowly, 'just how much I would come to need you.'

Feeling weak from this, the one and only intimation that she had done a good job for him, Jolene realised that she had better do something to counteract that weakness, and to get herself together. 'I slaved for you!' She saw no reason, in this moment of opposing weakening forces, to hide her light under a bushel.

'I know you did,' he said gently. 'But that wasn't what I meant.'

What he had meant, Jolene was very interested to know. But suddenly she was beset by nerves, and starting to be afraid. It had been madness to invite him in. She was already beginning to feel weak where he was concerned, and he had not been in her home ten minutes! Having been made to discount her original thought that he had come to boost her career, she as yet had no idea of the purpose of his call. But if ten minutes of his company could bring about such weakness in her, she felt she had real cause to panic should he, with his suddenly gentle tone, be minded to stay anywhere near the 'all day' he had intimated on her doorstep. The time had come, she decided, to find out what he was doing in Priors Aston and to edge him nearer to the door.

'Well—er—I wasn't working hard all the time,' she said as, trying to look casual, she got to her feet and inspected a potted plant her neighbour had given her yesterday.

'But even so, you felt too tired to come into the office this morning?' Cheyne, ever the gentleman as she'd hoped, got to his feet too.

'It wasn't that,' she said, feeling relieved as she took a step nearer to the door. 'It was just that—well . . .' she paused, and had a beautiful lie, that was not a lie, drop on to her tongue, 'just that I've no office to go to.'

'Ah,' said Cheyne, and when she looked at him, suddenly, he smiled.

'What does that "Ah" mean?' she questioned stiltedly, and felt she wanted to run when, before she could get the door open, he had taken a couple of long strides over to where she stood.

'From where I'm viewing things,' he replied, looking down into her eyes, 'I'd say that either you're nervous about—something—or you've given up all thoughts of a career.'

'Nervous?' she scoffed. 'Good grief!' she scorned, and was glad he could not see the mass of agitation she was inside when he moved that half-pace required which successfully prevented her from opening the door. 'And of course I haven't given up my thoughts of a career,' she said stoutly.

'Then why, if you're so career-minded—when, apart from me personally telling you to apply for Gillian's job when it comes up, you must know that the excellent work you did while we were away could only enhance your chances of promotion—did you not come in to work this morning?'

About to reiterate that she had no office to go to, Jolene saw then that her bluff had been called. But, with her way of escape barred, she had to think fast. 'I didn't know then that . . . Well, that is to say,' she floundered, 'that—well, I didn't know then . . . we—er—hadn't established then that . . .'

'I think what you're trying to say,' Cheyne cut in mildly, 'is that we've only just now agreed that my firm doesn't do business via the bedroom.'

'Yes, that's—about it,' Jolene accepted his helping her out gratefully.

'Which means,' he smiled pleasantly, 'that you must be quite ready to put your coat on and come to the office with me now.'

Heartily Jolene wished he would move away from the door—from her. She just could not think clearly with him standing so close. 'I don't think so,' she said stiffly.

'Why not?' he questioned, just the way she knew too late that he would, his eyes alert, watchful, never leaving her face.

'Because...' she tried, and, floundering again, and not liking the sensation, she was glad to feel rebellion surging to life in her. This was her home, for goodness' sake! Who in blazes did he think he was, to calmly force her to invite him in and then, for no good reason that she could see, proceed to make her squirm? 'It's not important, surely!' she broke out of her retreating mould to challenge sharply. And, as a big hint that she had had more than enough of his company, she stretched out a hand to the door-handle, and told him with some asperity, 'I'm sure you've far more important matters awaiting you at your desk.'

Suddenly, though, the whole of her being started to tingle, for Cheyne's right hand had unexpectedly stretched out, and all at once the hand she held over the doorknob was covered by his larger one. And, if that was not enough, she was abruptly feeling too electrified to move when, after a moment's pause during which he took a long-drawn breath, Cheyne was shattering her when he said, oh, so quietly, 'Believe me, Joley, there's nothing more important, nor that matters more to me, than being here with you, to...' He broke off and seemed to be searching for the right words.

But, shaken to her foundations at his tone, and at the beautiful way he had shortened her name, as he had done once before, she recalled without effort, all Jolene could do was to stare at him. Strangely, then, she had the most peculiar sensation that he seemed to be experiencing some of the same nervousness that she was feeling. But she discounted that Cheyne could be nervous of anything when, for all she sensed that she was not going to do herself any good, she just had to question, 'Why?'

For long, long moments he stared deep into her eyes, then he took another long-drawn breath, and was saying, 'Perhaps, considering what an uncommunicative swine I've been to you, I should first explain...'

He had again broken off but, never having expected to hear him admit that he had been an uncommunicative swine, or even that he had been aware of how he had been, much less that he would deign to explain anything to her, Jolene continued to stare at him. It was only afterwards, however, that she realised just how his words had shaken her. Because all at once she found that with his hand on her arm he had led her to her settee and had sat down with her—all with her barely being aware that she had moved.

Then, turning to her, he looked seriously, solemnly down into her wide green eyes and said, 'I've told you how aware I've been of you from the beginning. I've told you how I knew at Heathrow that I was going to have trouble with you. What I didn't know, however— and didn't have so much as an inkling of at the time— was the full extent of the trouble you were going to cause me when I made that decision not to leave you behind.'

'How, for goodness' sake?' asked Jolene with some heat. 'I don't recall doing anything to...'

'That's just it, my dear,' he cut her off gently, that 'my dear', not to mention his gentle tone, causing the heat of anger to depart immediately, 'you didn't have to do anything but be yourself to cause me trouble.'

'Compliments yet!' she tried to jibe, but her voice came out more husky than jibing.

'I haven't complimented you half enough,' Cheyne said softly, which did absolutely nothing to help her get the stiffening she needed.

'You told me I was beautiful—er—inside and out,' she attempted to drawl loftily.

'And so you are,' he promptly weakened her again by saying. 'All too soon,' he went on, 'I was seeing a very different Miss Jolene Draper from the one I'd initially decided you must be.'

'You realised that I wasn't some man-mad, marriage-wrecking hussy?' she queried as sourly as she could manage.

'Oh, yes,' he confirmed, but added wryly, 'Though that didn't stop me being bloody-minded each time I heard a whisper that you were going off somewhere with one of the others.'

'I . . .' Jolene began, faltered, then asked, 'When?'

'The list was ever growing,' he told her. 'It began that very first evening. No sooner had we landed, it seemed, than Shaw was making plans to take you to have a look around Red Square.'

'But Alec Edwards was going too!' she recalled, and did not have to dig much further into her memory to recall also 'But anyhow, I couldn't have gone with them because you said you wanted to brief me on...' her voice faded, and quickly she looked into the dark grey eyes that were still alert, and still watching her.

'All along it had been my intention to brief you at breakfast the following morning,' he told her, to her astonishment.

'But why stop me going out with Keith and Alec?' she said when she had some breath back. 'Oh!' she exclaimed as the reason came to her. 'You weren't sure that early on that I wasn't the marriage-breaker...'

'I gave myself all sorts of reasons but the right one,' Cheyne cut in quietly, and added, 'I buried my head in the sand for quite some time, I'm afraid.'

'Did you?' she queried, and was no longer wondering what Cheyne was doing there in her sitting-room, because she felt so surrounded in fog, suddenly, that she was more concerned with hoping he could clear some of that fog away.

'I did,' he said, and set her heart wildly racing when he smiled, and added, 'When your beauty started to get to me, I told myself that I'd seen beauty before. When a feeling of wanting to protect you came over me, I was able to rationalise that, as your employer, how else should I feel?'

'I—er—see,' she murmured, seeing nothing, the fog still as thick.

'Which is more than I could at the time,' he told her. 'For all I told myself that as I was your "protective" employer it was natural that I should be filled with rage when I saw Shaw coming out of your room in Irkutsk buttoning his shirt—*that*, I later realised, was not the true reason.'

'It—wasn't?' Jolene asked chokily, clearly remembering how Cheyne had looked on the morning when she had sewed a button on Keith's shirt, and they had left her room together.

'It was not,' he confirmed, and went on to make her heart race even more wildly when, looking into her eyes, he told her quietly, 'Something very serious was happening to me, Jolene Draper.'

'S-something—to do—w-with me?' she managed to get out jerkily, afraid to think, afraid to feel, and suddenly feeling too confused to do anything but keep her eyes fixed firmly on him.

'Everything to do with you,' he confirmed. 'There was I, all hard-headed businessman taking a tour round a Russian factory in connection with a joint venture which means a lot to me—then what happens?' Dumbly she looked at him and with a wry look Cheyne went on, 'You happen. There I am, thoroughly absorbed in the latest Russian technology, when suddenly I get a glimpse of you doing your damnedest not to yawn, and when a week earlier I'd have been furious with you, suddenly I'm finding I'm hard put to it not to grin stupidly at you.'

'I remember...' Jolene said dreamily, then she remembered something else. 'You weren't having any trouble later on that day,' she reminded him. 'You...' Her voice faded when Cheyne frowned, and it seemed that she had no need to remind him of anything.

'I should smile on pleasantly while at lunch you sit there enjoying Viktor Sekirkin making sheep's eyes at you?' he questioned, a harsh note coming to his voice for the first time in an age—quite clearly, he had forgotten nothing.

'That's a bit strong, isn't it?' she roused herself to argue. 'We were there to do business; I could hardly ignore the man!'

'I suppose not,' Cheyne conceded, and smiled slightly self-ashamedly as he said, 'See what you do to me? The man isn't even around, and still I'm jealous of him!'

'*Jealous!*' Jolene exclaimed, her heart thundering anew when, looking nowhere but at Cheyne, she saw from the expression on his face that the word jealous seemed to have slipped out without him even knowing it.

But he did not deny it, and suddenly her heart was thundering so loudly that she thought he must hear it when he asked, 'Haven't you been listening to a word I've been saying? What else could it be but jealousy, that not once but several times I invented work for you so you shouldn't spend your time with any man but me?'

'You made me work that night—simply because you'd overheard Viktor ask me to ring him if I was free?' she asked incredulously.

'Without thinking about it twice,' Cheyne admitted, entirely without shame, though he did qualify, 'Naturally I told myself at the time that I wanted that dictation out of my head so that I could get on with something else.'

'But it w-wasn't true?' she stammered, feeling suddenly so mixed up inside, so vulnerable, that she did not know whether she wanted Cheyne to stop before he said any more, or whether she wanted him to go on; or what she wanted to happen.

'It was not,' he answered her, then went on, 'Forgive the way I've been with you, but having gone to Russia with my thoughts meant to be solely on work, I was all too soon making new discoveries about myself—and about you—that in turn have given me one hell of a time.'

It was at that point that Jolene knew, although she had no idea where this conversation was leading, that she wanted to hear Cheyne out. He had turned her world on its head by stating, quite openly, that he had known jealousy over her, and, for good or ill, she then knew that she wanted to hear more about these new discoveries he had made.

'What sort—of discoveries?' she asked quietly, and was not left to wonder much longer when Cheyne replied,

'About you—that you were all that you outwardly appeared to be,' he said softly, with his dark grey eyes warm on the wide green eyes that stared at him. 'About myself...?' he shrugged, then said, 'So many firsts.'

'Firsts?' she queried, and Cheyne nodded.

'We were about to board a plane in Omsk when as I looked at you and your entranced expression as you stared at the superb sunset, for the first time in my life my breath suddenly felt strangled within me.'

'I remember,' Jolene said in a hushed kind of voice, 'That is...' she got herself a little together to explain '...I r-remember it being a—um—breathless kind of moment.'

'For you too?' he asked, but nerves were attacking her again, and she could not answer his question.

'You s-said there were many firsts,' she attempted to deflect his question instead, and Cheyne smiled an understanding smile which only served to make her more nervous because she was not certain that she wanted him understanding anything of why she would want to evade his questions.

She forgot some of her nervousness, however, when he surprised her by seeming ready to answer everything she wanted to know, and resumed, 'There are you, a young woman who I'd observed could look impudent without ever saying an impudent word. Here am I, too busy with my thoughts of work to wonder how I feel inside, when suddenly I discover that you have the ability to make me feel good inside.'

'I do?' Jolene could not prevent the question from escaping.

'You do,' he confirmed readily. 'You, I discovered, my dear, had the power to amuse me, when I was sure you shouldn't. You, sweet one, have the ability to make me laugh and to smile when only moments before I've seen nothing to laugh or to smile at.' She was still in a seventh heaven of wonder at his 'my dear' and at his 'sweet one', when Cheyne went on, 'Through you, and for the first time in my life, I've been aware of raw, naked jealousy.'

'Because of—Keith and Alec?' she questioned, and was not surprised that she had got it slightly wrong when Cheyne replied,

'Of course Keith and Alec. Though the main culprit was Sekirkin and the way you'd gone behind my back to phone him and tell him you'd returned to Irkutsk and had an afternoon free.'

'I didn't telephone him!' Jolene denied, and at Cheyne's straight look that said he had seen her with the Russian himself that afternoon, 'He must have been in the hotel on some business or other, and spotted me when I was at the Beriozka buying some gifts to bring home,' she explained. 'You'd said you didn't need me that afternoon, and...'

'I believe you, Joley,' Cheyne cut her off gently, and smiled as gently too he added. 'I had, as you say, told you that I didn't need you—but only to start to realise then that I was growing to need you very much.'

At his words, his gentleness, the almost tender expression on his face, Jolene's heart gave another erratic burst. 'You were—growing to need me—because of—work?' she asked in a fractured kind of voice, and was suddenly breathless again when, before replying, Cheyne gently took hold of both her hands in his.

'My need for you has nothing whatever to do with work,' he told her sincerely.

'It—hasn't?' she questioned, her question barely audible.

She was gripping his hands tightly when, tenderly, he asked, 'Have you not seen how it is with me, my dear one?'

'Oh, Cheyne,' was wrenched from her nervously.

And it was as if he had observed her nervousness, for, 'Sweet love,' he breathed softly, 'I'm afraid you've captured my heart.'

'Oh—Cheyne!' she cried once more, and with her heart thundering against her ribs, she could only stare shiny-eyed at him.

'Does—that mean that you care for me in return?' he asked, and there was a trace of hesitation in his voice as though he was afraid to hope for too much. 'Have I misread the signs completely?' he asked, his voice taking on an urgency as he questioned quickly, 'Do you not feel anything for me?' And, when she had thought that he had forgotten about the painting which she had purchased in Leningrad, 'Was I totally wrong to gain encouragement when you tried to get me to take my mind off the fact that you've got a picture of "our place" on your wall?'

'Our place?' queried Jolene, selecting that question out of all he was asking.

'Can you deny that the painting puts you in mind of the village of St Nicholas—the place where I, and I think you, knew an hour of perfect happiness?'

'You felt it too?' she choked.

'Never in my life have I ever felt so at one with any person.'

Jolene very nearly breathed his name again. But suddenly, vividly, she was remembering that it had not taken him long to change into a surly brute who could barely spare a word for her.

'What happened?' she questioned, and when he looked a degree mystified by her question, 'At dinner that night, you...'

She did not have to go on. 'What a lot you have to forgive me for,' he stated. 'Will you try to understand if I tell you that nothing like this had ever happened to me before. I was there in the USSR to do business, not to feel like some weak-kneed out-of-control schoolkid because some beautiful, tantalising secretary is getting to me.'

Tantalising! Out of control! Jolene was so thrilled at the way in which Cheyne was opening up to her that she did not know which of the questions that queued up to ask first.

'You—out of control?' was the one that won.

'Believe it,' he smiled, and was still smiling as he reminisced, 'Never has any female made me so mad that I have to resort to physically laying my hands on her!'

'You're referring to that day in our hotel in Listvyanka when I hit you?' Jolene queried, feeling suddenly so at one with him that she immediately landed accurately, she saw as he nodded, on his wavelength.

'No way had it been in my mind to kiss you,' he confessed. 'But that was before I touched you. And, once

I'd put my hands on your arms, and looked into your defiant eyes, something just came over me. I kissed you, felt you warm and lovely in my arms, and was just finding some trace of will-power to take my arms from around you when you began to push me away. I spent the afternoon alternately working on my speech for the Novosibirsk conference, and telling myself that this was no way for your employer to go on.'

'Yet the very next day, at the village of St Nicholas, you kissed me again.'

'And again, I hadn't meant to. You'd told me the previous evening at dinner that you'd got no reason to hurry back to England, and I, naturally without knowing it, translated that to mean that you weren't attached to any one male, and felt good about everything again. When down in our village you suddenly looked at me, all large eyes and adorable, I just had to know the taste of your sweet lips again.'

'Oh!' Jolene sighed, feeling that at last she was really getting to know something of the man she had given her heart to, and she smiled gently, and suggested, 'Which was why, of course, you were such an unbearable dinner companion that same evening.'

'Of course,' he replied, that slightly ashamed look which she was beginning to find endearing coming out again. 'Forces were at work within me, sweet Joley, about which I had no previous knowledge—can you wonder I was finding it difficult to cope? On the one hand I wanted you exclusively to myself, yet on the other I was pleased to be leaving Lake Baikal, and the peculiar influence it was having on me, to join Edwards and Shaw in Irkutsk. Then all at the same time, believe it or not, while I'm seriously considering cancelling our railway trip, those wanting-you-to-myself forces were at work staying my hand. I didn't like it in the least,' he confessed, 'when Sekirkin turned up at the railway station clutching a red rose in his amorous paw.'

'Mmm,' murmured Jolene as something occurred to her, 'it was you, wasn't it? You,' she went on to enlighten him, 'who took that rose from its . . .' she had no need to continue.

'I wasn't having that thing stuck under my nose all day,' Cheyne told her in no uncertain fashion. 'I told you,' he reminded her gently, 'that jealousy had got to me.'

'Did you know then that—you—er—I'd—er—c-captured your heart?'

'There's nothing so blind as a man who won't see, my dear,' he replied gently. 'All the signs were there, but when you're thirty-seven and have never felt that way before, a certain stubborn refusal to face facts suddenly gets in the way. So at that time all I was admitting to was that Viktor Sekirkin annoyed me intensely, but that so too did you when you kicked up a fuss about wanting a four-berth compartment all to yourself. Only for my annoyance to go flying, though, when after having totally disturbed my equilibrium, you suddenly smiled and I couldn't help thinking that your smile was like sunshine after rain.'

'We sat and just talked away the afternoon,' Jolene recalled quietly.

'We did,' Cheyne agreed. 'And, without putting it into words even to myself, I knew I was happy. The feeling, I knew,' he went on, 'had its roots in being in your company, and I knew that I didn't want to lose sight of you. Is it any wonder that while we were having dinner that night I should realise that I wanted to see you every day?'

'Really?' Jolene breathed, her heart pounding capriciously from all that he was saying.

'Depend on it,' he murmured, though he then owned, 'At that point I was still stubbornly holding out against admitting what had happened to me. In my superior wisdom I was telling myself that since I wanted to see you every day, it must be because I found your work so faultless that I instinctively knew that you'd be a fine replacement for Gillian.'

'Which is why you suggested I apply for her job,' Jolene put in.

'Exactly,' Cheyne confirmed, and smiled as he added, 'Little did I know that the truth was just around the corner waiting to deliver a sledgehammer blow!'

'After dinner?' she queried, her hands absently clutching at his hands.

'After you'd turned in for the night,' he told her, and that gentleness was there again when, moving one of his hands to cup the right side of her face, he told her, 'I'd discovered that you were, as you'd once angrily told me, a virgin, and while you were able to laugh, I was too stunned to laugh. Thoughts of you, though, kept me sleepless, and I was coming nearer and nearer to knowing what was in my heart when, as I stared unseeing out of the compartment's window, the train suddenly came to an abrupt and jerky halt, and...'

'And you fell on to my bed,' Jolene remembered.

'I did, and we touched, and having touched it was like a bolt of electricity going through me. Forgive me, my dear, but for some minutes I went totally out of control. You were in my arms, warm, wonderful, and responding. Then, as suddenly as it had stopped, the train was starting off again. And in between the stopping and the starting, I knew that I was in love with you.'

Jolene's breath caught in her throat. 'You—you're in love with me?' she questioned in a choked and croaky voice, only to have Cheyne move both his hands to place them on her shoulders.

'You really *haven't* been listening,' he scolded her gently. Then, with exquisite tenderness, he drew her that bit closer to him, then with a thistledown touch, he kissed both corners of her mouth. 'I love you dearly, sweet Joley,' he said in an emotion-filled voice, and, with his serious grey eyes deeply intent on hers, 'Am I completely wrong to hope that you have some feeling—for me?' he asked.

Before she could speak Jolene had to swallow hard to clear a sudden constriction in her throat. 'No,' she managed to answer him huskily, 'You're—not wrong.'

'You—care for me a little?' Cheyne pressed.

'I care for you—a lot,' she replied, and while her heart was beating wildly from all she was hearing, those strong, firm hands on her shoulders hauled her right up against him.

'Oh, my dear, dear love,' he murmured in a low voice, as pulling back he again looked deeply into her eyes as if to convince himself that she was speaking the truth. 'You love me?' he insisted.

'Very much,' she told him shyly, and all was quiet in the room for some long minutes while Cheyne alternately held her fast to him, then put some space between them so that he could look into her eyes. And then at last, he kissed her.

But one kiss was not enough, and it was many kisses later that he pulled back to look into her love-filled eyes, and to smile gently at the warm pink in her cheeks from the emotion he had aroused in her.

'Dear love,' he breathed, his look almost reverent as, keeping an arm about her, he took hold of her hand with his free hand, and added, 'I want everything to be so right for you.'

'You do?' she smiled.

'I do,' he replied, and thrilled her to the core of her being when he went on to tell her, 'Can you wonder that I don't know what in thunder is happening to me when, as wide apart as a day, yet as close as the next second, I've in turn been furious with you, yet wanting to cut my tongue out if I've hurt your feelings. I've been admiring of your spirit, yet ready to take you to task for impertinence. I've known jealousy over you, and, to crown it all, when I've wanted most desperately to make love to you, I've discovered such a need in me to protect you that somehow I've managed to find the control to leave you.'

'Oh, Cheyne,' she said softly, and was gently kissed again. Just as gently, he broke his kiss, and as he looked at her and seemed in no hurry to look away, Jolene only then realised that, for all she had pushed him away from her on the train, had he refused to be pushed away, then most surely their lovemaking would have ended in a very different way. 'It was on the train, wasn't it?' she smiled.

'It was,' he smiled adoringly back. 'I'd just realised that I was in love with you, and then everything seemed to happen together. One moment I was in love and desiring you like crazy, and then the next something was telling me—no, not like this, not in a bunk that's barely big enough for one, let alone two—it just wasn't right for you. I got out as fast as I could, and spent the rest of that fateful night out in the corridor thinking about you, and how it had been. The more I thought about it, though, the more I realised that as I went to pull back from you, you had tried to push me away. It was a nightmare,' he ended, 'wondering, had I scared you half to death?'

'Oh, no,' she disclaimed promptly, and as Cheyne found a grin she smiled shyly at how forward that had sounded. Though she did feel bound to confess, 'I did panic a little, I admit, but that was only because—well, I'd had a bad experience when I was sixteen and...'

'*Oh, dear lord!*' Cheyne cut in, sounding utterly appalled. 'My poor darling!' he cried, and held her to him for several moments before he asked quietly, 'Can you tell me about it?'

'Oh, yes,' she told him, making her voice purposely light when Cheyne was looking as though her pain was his pain. 'My parents are super,' she prefixed what she was going to say, 'but, probably because I'm an only child, they brought me up in a very sheltered way. Anyhow,' she went on swiftly, 'I don't think I was a very clued-up sixteen-year-old, so that when the lustful shop owner at my Saturday job cornered me one Saturday and told me in a lewd way that he'd always fancied a virgin I just didn't have the nous to call his bluff, but was so terrified that I hit him with a brush I'd grabbed hold of, and then bolted.'

'My poor, poor sweetheart!' Cheyne cradled her to him, and was still holding her gently to him when a few minutes later, he probed tenderly, 'Has that experience frightened you from sharing yourself, dear love?'

Pulling a little away from him, Jolene shook her head. 'To be truthful, I did wonder once or twice when I couldn't—er—get very enthusiastic about any of the men I've dated. And then,' she said shyly, 'I met you.'

'And then...?' Cheyne probed further, but she could see that his mouth was starting to turn up encouragingly at the corners, and she knew that although there was seriousness behind his question in that he wanted no dark secrets between them, there was some teasing there too.

'And then,' she obliged, 'while I panicked briefly, feeling that you, like him, only wanted... well, anyway, I panicked and pushed at you. But as soon as that brief dart of panic had gone...' her eyes suddenly grew round and innocent, '... I wanted you back with me again. I,' she said, 'discovered that night that I'm just as normal as the next woman.'

It seemed natural then that they should kiss and cling to each other, and as Cheyne's arms tightened about her, Jolene held him closely to her.

'I love you, sweet love,' Cheyne said in a throaty, husky voice, when at last they broke apart, and tracing a forefinger over the line of her bottom lip, 'When did you know that you loved me?' he wanted to know.

'Remember "our" village?' she smiled.

'Since then?' he asked incredulously.

Happily Jolene nodded. 'Though, like you, I was aware before then.'

'What—even while I was being such a tight-lipped swine to you?'

'Both before and after,' she chuckled. 'Though...' she hesitated.

'What, my darling?' he asked. 'We belong to each other now,' he went on to thrill her to her very soul, 'there's nothing you can't ask me that I won't answer.'

'Oh, Cheyne!' she breathed, and, purely because she could not help it, she reached up and kissed him.

'I think I'm going to enjoy belonging to you,' he told her tenderly, and smiling, he asked, 'So what was the question?'

'Why...' she grinned, suddenly feeling that she really could ask him anything, '...why, when you knew, on the train, that you were in love with me, did you behave as if I didn't matter to you at all?'

'For another first, sweetheart,' he replied promptly, 'I discovered that I, who in my day have, without turning a hair, signed deals which have committed my company to spending millions, was suddenly knotted up with nerves because I didn't know what, if anything at all, you felt for me.'

'You—knotted up with nerves!' she exclaimed, thunderstruck.

'If *you're* surprised, imagine how *I* felt!' he responded. 'Suddenly I'm aware of an electric charge that happens whenever I touch you, so that when, the day before, while I found it quite pleasurable to hold your hand as I helped you from each coach to the train's restaurant coach, all at once I'm too nervous to so much as hold your hand in case I lose control again.'

'Good lord!' she gasped in astonishment.

'You can say that again,' he smiled lovingly. 'That morning on that train seemed to go on forever. I was never more glad than when it pulled into Novosibirsk.'

'Ah,' said Jolene, and when Cheyne looked enquiringly at her, she too did not want any dark secrets between them. 'That was where you went straight into the arms of Lyudmila Antipova and I,' she smiled, 'for the first time in *my* life, knew what jealousy feels like.'

'Seriously?' Cheyne exclaimed.

'Seriously,' she replied, and they both burst out laughing when she told him, 'There's no need to look so delighted!'

His delighted look had disappeared, however, when he went on to explain how, because of his love for her and the anxiety of not knowing if she felt anything for him, he had begun having trouble with his usual single-mindedness about his work.

'You're saying that I started to get in the way of your work?' Jolene queried.

'And how!' he replied. 'Which is why I had to make the decision to leave everything between you and me on hold until I'd got the work we were in Russia to do out of the way. I would by far have preferred to concentrate on finding out how things were with you,' he confided, 'but instead I had to put up with a strained relationship with you which seemed to be gouging an even wider gap between us. Though I came close to folding on Thursday, in Leningrad,' he revealed.

'When?' Jolene wanted to know, and learned that it had been when she had taken some typing to him. He had been fighting hard not to haul her into his room to talk to her, when she had asked him if he wanted her for anything, and he had replied, 'Nothing that I can think of.'

'I saw hurt in your eyes,' he went on, 'and called after you, but you weren't in any mood to hear, and I let you go because I was then unsure that you had looked hurt. But when I was aching like hell for some heart's ease, that stray belief that I'd seen hurt in your eyes gave me hope that perhaps you did care a little.'

'Oh, my love,' broke from Jolene, 'I didn't know it was as bad as that for you too!'

'Murder is understating it,' he replied, but he had a smile for her as he went on, 'Then, just as we're coming to the end of our work, what happens but that we're in Moscow again, and Shaw and Edwards are back on the scene.'

'And you're jealous again?' she guessed.

'Who wouldn't be?' he grumbled nicely. 'Although I'm trying to convince myself that I might have some faint chance with you, all I'm getting is a load of grief. Yet no sooner do you see that pair than it's all laughter and smiles—for them. Can you wonder that I lost no time in finding you some work when you couldn't wait to accept another of Shaw's invitations to look round Red Square with them?'

'You mean you *deliberately* found me some *unnecessary* work to...'

'I'm sorry, sweetheart,' Cheyne took over when her voice faded in shock. 'If you want to see St Basil's Cathedral, or Gums, or anywhere else, I'll take you any time you say. But not then. Then, I confess, it was more than I could take to let you go...'

'You deliberately gave me that most boring, most horrendous, most...'

'Most foul piece of mind-blowing nonsense I've ever conceived,' admitted Cheyne freely. 'But only to be filled with such compunction, when, looking so adorable, so innocent, you brought that immaculately typed report back to me, that with my heart suddenly starting to hammer I came within an ace of telling you just how very much I loved you.'

'Oh, Cheyne!' she sighed, and felt weak inside about him. 'What stopped you?' she asked.

'The floor attendant chose that moment to walk by,' he replied. 'It gave me pause to realise that if I was hoping to win you, now was not the time. In fact,' he went on, 'I was by that time getting so uptight about you that, having firmly come to the conclusion that our work must first be finished, immediately we landed in England—work at an end—the impulse not to let you out of my sight has me blurting out like some callow youth that I'll give you a lift home.'

'I'm sorry I refused,' Jolene smiled, but had to ask, 'Was it your intention to ask me to come and see you in your office today?'

'It was my intention, after all the time-switching we've been doing, to let you have a decent night's rest, and then to come and see you on Sunday,' he corrected her.

'Sunday—yesterday?' she exclaimed, and he nodded.

'The only trouble with that idea, my darling,' he told her ruefully, 'was that, to my astonishment, I discovered that I didn't know where you lived. Why aren't you in the phone book?' he demanded, and because she couldn't help it, Jolene just gurgled with laughter.

'Because my parents only finally gave me their blessing about my leaving home when I agreed to go ex-directory,' she told him happily, realising that if he could not find her number in the book, he would not be able to find her address either.

'Hmph,' he grunted. 'You do appreciate, I hope, that but for a last-minute moment of sanity returning, I very nearly got Raven into the office to open up his personnel files yesterday.'

'You didn't!' she exclaimed with saucer-wide eyes.

'It was a close call,' Cheyne smiled. 'See what you do to me, young woman!' he said mock-severely. 'I couldn't wait to get to the office this morning, I was so impatient to see you. I couldn't believe it when my enquiries revealed that you were nowhere in the building.'

'Oh, Cheyne!' she sighed, and just had to add, 'I do so love you.'

Firmly he gathered her into his arms and tenderly placed a kiss on her brow, then quietly he asked her, 'Do you have any more questions, my dear heart?'

As she stared up into the warm depths of his dark grey eyes, Jolene's heart gave a flutter of pure joy. 'No, Cheyne, I haven't,' she told him.

Gently he kissed her mouth. His eyes were adoring on her large green eyes. 'Then may I ask one?' he enquired.

'Of course,' she said softly, 'anything.'

'Then, my dear, since I love you to distraction and can't bear you out of my sight, when are you going to marry me?' he asked.

'Oh, Cheyne!' Jolene sighed, and just before their lips met, 'Quite soon, I hope,' she answered tremulously.

HARLEQUIN

Coming Next Month

#3067 ANOTHER MAN'S RING Angela Carson
Judi knows she doesn't want to marry Robert—but breaking it off won't be
easy. A job offer in Thailand provides an escape, until she realizes that
working for Nick Compton, she's jumped from the frying pan into the fire!

#3068 LOVE'S RANSOM Dana James
Zanthi enjoys her diplomatic post as assistant secretary on a small Caribbean
island—but she senses something very odd is happening. Especially when
surveyor Garran Crossley arrives and she is assigned to accompany him on his
land survey....

#3069 THE TURQUOISE HEART Ellen James
Annie Brooke travels to New Mexico to restore a damaged painting for
Derrek Richards. A simple job, she thinks. But the feelings Derrek arouses in
Annie's heart are far from simple....

#3070 A MATTER OF PRINCIPAL Leigh Michaels
Patrick's job is to sort out Camryn's finances—but he is threatening her whole
way of life. To protect herself and her young daughter, Camryn has to fight
him, though he proves difficult to resist—both as a banker and as a man!

#3071 HILLTOP TRYST Betty Neels
Oliver Latimer is safe and reassuring, and Beatrice is glad he was there to pick
up the pieces when her life turned upside down. Against Colin Ward's charm,
however, Oliver seems to have nothing to offer—until Beatrice takes a good
second look....

#3072 A SUMMER KIND OF LOVE Shannon Waverly
Recently widowed, Joanna Ingalls needs a quiet summer alone with her five-
year-old son. But when they arrive at her father's cottage, she's shocked to
find Michael Malone living there—the man she'd loved so desperately six
years before.

Available in August wherever paperback books are sold, or through
Harlequin Reader Service:

In the U.S.
901 Fuhrmann Blvd.
P.O. Box 1397
Buffalo, N.Y. 14240-1397

In Canada
P.O. Box 603
Fort Erie, Ontario
L2A 5X3

COMING SOON

In August, two worlds will collide in four very special romance titles. Somewhere between first meeting and happy ending, Dreamscape Romance will sweep you to the very edge of reality where everyday reason cannot conquer unlimited imagination—or the power of love. The timeless mysteries of reincarnation, telepathy, psychic visions and earthbound spirits intensify the modern lives and passion of ordinary men and women with an extraordinary alluring force.

Available next month!

EARTHBOUND—Rebecca Flanders
THIS TIME FOREVER—Margaret Chittenden
MOONSPELL—Regan Forest
PRINCE OF DREAMS—Carly Bishop

DRSC